# IT CRAWLED CLOSER
# AND CLOSER . . .

Like a monstrous shining insect, the locomotive towered high and black above them, its tall stack shutting out the stars. The rusted tip of the train's thrusting metal cowcatcher gently nudged the toe of Ventry's right boot as the incredible night mammoth slid to a final grinding stop.

A red glow emanated from the steamer's interior. A door in the first passenger coach, directly behind the coal car, opened like a dark wound.

Inviting them in . . .

# HELLTRACKS

**WILLIAM F. NOLAN**

AVON BOOKS ◆ NEW YORK

Portions of this novel, in different form, first appeared in the October 1981 issue of *Gallery* as "The Train," in the Summer 1988 issue of *The Horror Show* as "The Cure," and from Deadline Publications in 1991 as "Blood Sky."

HELLTRACKS is an original publication of Avon Books. This work has never before appeared in book form. This work is a novel. Any similarity to actual persons or events is purely coincidental.

AVON BOOKS
A division of
The Hearst Corporation
1350 Avenue of the Americas
New York, New York 10019

Copyright © 1991 by William F. Nolan
Cover illustration by James Warren
Published by arrangement with the author
Library of Congress Catalog Card Number: 91–92053
ISBN: 0-380-75746-X

First Avon Books Printing: November 1991

AVON TRADEMARK REG. U.S. PAT. OFF. AND IN OTHER COUNTRIES, MARCA REGISTRADA, HECHO EN U.S.A.

Printed in the U.S.A.

RA 10 9 8 7 6 5 4 3 2 1

To the best person I know,
my wife,
**Cameron Nolan**
with continued love
and with special thanks
for her valuable contributions
to this book.

*Each of us follows a track in life,
for good or evil. These tracks can
take us to fame and success, or they
can take us to horror and despair.
Some are truly hellish . . .
and they all end in death.*

—Hans Paytr Mannheim

*It was feeding.*

*Deep in the inked blackness of its lair, shielded from the raw glare of mountain sunlight, its daggered teeth ripped at the still-warm flesh of its prey. At tendon and juiced muscle, digging for the marrow, gorging itself.*

*A spitting sound—as it disgorged its final morsel.*

*A skull, eyeless and stark, tooth-scored along the occipital bone.*

*A human skull.*

# 1

PAUL VENTRY OPENED HIS EYES IN THE DARKNESS. He didn't want to get up, but he knew that further sleep was impossible. The sun was still well below the Little Belt, and the bedroom was dim and cold. Ventry had always been a light sleeper. As a child he had invariably awakened before his two younger brothers, and was the first to appear, eager-eyed and wolf-hungry, at the long wooden table for morning chow. In those days, for young Paul, life was a daily adventure.

While his brothers often complained about the backbreaking ranch work in the glare-sun summers and bitter Montana winters, Paul reveled in it. Their father, Dave Ventry, had marketed the finest wool in Madison Valley. He was a sheep man, born and bred, and young Paul had set out, from a very early age, to follow David Ventry's example. He had all but worshipped the tall, craggy figure who had taught him everything there was to know about sheep ranching.

And, indeed, Paul had made his father proud of him; he had carried on the Ventry tradition, marketing the finest Rambouillet wool on Big Moccasin. Despite the steady decline of sheep ranching in this part of the state over recent decades, the Ventry herds retained their reputation as "top of the line."

But now he was questioning all of it. Lying here in his bed in the predawn chill of a morning in early September, Paul

Ventry felt no pride in what he had accomplished; he felt only pain and emptiness.

The pain of loss.

Before Sarrie had become ill, the old fires had still burned within him. Even in his fifties, the challenges of life as a Montana sheepman had continued to stir and excite him.

Until the cancer. Until the specialist in Billings told them there was no hope for his wife, that no operation was possible. The disease had raged through Sarah Ventry like a wind-driven brushfire, taking her away from him forever.

Ventry's hand traced the empty space on the bed where she had slept each night for so many years.

Sarrie had been gone for almost three months now, with the damned cancer taking her at the outset of her favorite season, when the spring chinooks had come and gone, when the passing of those south winds had prepared the earth for a flood of riotous color. As a girl, growing up on a neighboring ranch in western Montana (long before they'd fallen in love, married, and started their own ranch in the central part of the state), Sarrie had a deep affinity for that season—the end of spring and the beginning of summer. She'd ride the hills over a rich carpet of dogtooth violets, crocuses and forget-me-nots, savoring the wild iris and the evening primrose.

They'd met in those hills thirty-five years ago, when he was twenty and she was eighteen.

Ventry got up, walked slowly downstairs. Even with Josh and Amy living in the house, it seemed empty to him without Sarrie. He loved both of his children, but it wasn't the same. Couldn't be. The death of his parents had been tough to bear, but they were in the natural order of things. Sarrie's death was an open wound that Paul Ventry was afraid would never heal.

He was just finishing breakfast when his daughter entered the kitchen. The sun had cleared the peaks of the Little Belt, and as she walked toward him, Amy's face looked golden in the early morning light. She reminded Ventry, once again, of a young fawn, delicate and lovely, and the fresh sight of her made him feel ashamed of his dark thoughts.

"Morning, Dad," she said, leaning to give him a peck on the cheek. "Any orange juice left?"

"Plenty," said Ventry.

She poured herself a glass from the carton, sitting down next to him at the table.

"I miss the old days when we all ate breakfast together," she said. "Like a family."

"That was your mother's doing," said Ventry. "She loved fixing big ranch breakfasts, seeing you and me and Josh all digging in."

He stared down at the table.

A silence between them. Just the metallic ticking of the wall clock. Amy touched her father's hand.

"I know how much you miss her," she said. "I do, too." She pressed his hand. "I didn't mean to—"

"It's okay, honey," said Ventry, pushing back his plate. He stood up and a shaft of sun struck him at shoulder level, accenting the hard, ridged face, dominated by the fierce blue of his eyes.

Amy had her mother's green eyes, equally intense, framed by her short-cut red hair. At twenty, she reminded Paul Ventry of a young colt, frisky, a little wild, but full of future promise. He thought often of what kind of mother she'd make, of what her own children, his grandchildren, would be like.

He rinsed his coffee mug in the sink. "I drink too damn much of this stuff."

"Another herder's quitting," said Amy. "Ernie Collard's going to open a tire store in Helena."

Ventry's face tightened. "Ernie's gonna sell *tires*! What the hell does a sheepherder know about tires?"

"C'mon, Dad, Ernie's just being realistic," she said. "Sheepherders are—"

"I know, I know. A vanishing breed—as you and Josh keep telling me."

"All of the other ranchers on Big Moccasin use copters for most of their herding."

"Scares hell out of the sheep," snapped Ventry.

She smiled, shaking her head. "Dad, we're practically into the twenty-first century. You keep acting like this is still 1880.

Montana's changed a lot. It isn't really sheep country any-more. Not the way it used to be."

"Are we going to start all this again?" Ventry asked sourly. "About me being some kind of dinosaur in the space age?"

"I never called you a dinosaur. But you *are* a stubborn, old-fashioned man. You won't even *discuss* the idea of selling the ranch."

"I'm fifty-five. I've been sheep ranching all my life. I wouldn't know what else to do."

"At least you could streamline things, modernize more."

"Let's not go over this again. I'm as modern as I intend to get. Now, if you'll just fork that chow into your belly, we've got some lambs to round up."

And he left the kitchen.

# 2

THREE DOZEN LAMBS HAD BEEN LOST DURING THE previous day's drive from the upper ranges of the Little Belt. Early September was shipping season and the herders had successfully separated the lambs from their mothers in the high country, and had been driving them down to the corrals, when a thick morning fog swept in. It was almost impossible to keep the half-weaned, fractious animals from straying off in the fog, despite the best efforts of the herdsmen and their dogs.

When they reached the counting corrals at the foot of the mountains, some three dozen lambs were missing.

Accompanied by his son and daughter, Ventry was determined to find them.

It took the trio of riders two hours of hard climbing to reach the wild area where the sheep had been lost. Around them the trees were flushed with autumn gold: cottonwoods and aspens and willows burned against the grassed slope.

Ventry dismounted to study the ground, carefully scanning the terrain. He found the grass and weeds had been trampled to the north.

Frightened sheep will always run together. When they found one, they'd find them all.

They rode north.

Young Josh Ventry jogged alongside his father, easing himself in the saddle, pulling the big Stetson lower across his forehead.

"You sure they headed this way?"

"Signs don't lie," said Paul Ventry, eyes on the trail.

Josh was tall, like his father, with the same steel-blue eyes and wide sweep of shoulder. He was five years older than his sister, born the same winter Paul Ventry had sold their ranch near Sweet Grass Creek to purchase this smaller spread at the foot of the Little Belt Mountains. Josh recognized the flaws in his father—his ram-stubbornness, his inability to openly express parental love, his sometimes violent temper—but he felt great affection for this taciturn man, mixed with a certain degree of awe and respect at the legendary position his father held among ranchers throughout central Montana.

Josh had never considered another way of existence; when as a boy he'd been asked what profession he intended to pursue, his reply had always been quick and firm: "sheepman." He'd taken a lot of ribbing over the years from several of his more ambitious friends, but Josh Ventry had never wavered in his desire to make sheep ranching his life's work. The Ventry legacy was something to be proud of. Now and in the future.

Amy, on Rex, her pinto, had been trailing behind both men. She increased pace to draw alongside her brother as Paul Ventry opened a lead ahead of them.

"My throat's dry as a bone," she said. "I need to borrow your canteen."

Handing it over, he asked, "What happened to yours?"

"Empty." She took several swallows, then returned the canteen. "Thanks."

They rode on in silence, the mountains pressing in around them.

"You ever feel odd . . . riding up here?" Amy asked her brother.

"Odd how?"

"Like we really don't belong. Like the trees and the rocks and the sage . . . *they* all belong, but we don't?"

He threw her a grin. "You going mystical again?"

"There's a book I read," Amy continued. "About nature spirits. How the rocks and trees are living entities, and that each has a consciousness which is evolving just like *we're* evolving. And eventually the consciousness reaches some sort of critical vibratory rate, and at that point, what they have is a soul. A kind of newborn baby soul, which will just keep evolving until eventually it'll be something like a human soul.''

Josh looked at her, amused. "Well, I guess in a sense you could say that everything is alive—but I don't know about the 'soul' part.''

"This book said that there are special areas on earth—sacred places—where the forms of nature have the ability to reshape themselves, take on organic life.''

"Sounds a little far out to me,'' said Josh.

"The Indians considered the Little Belt Mountains to be a sacred place," she said. "They really believed in these things.''

"They also believed that animals could talk, but I've never had a conversation with my horse.''

"Indian beliefs are fascinating," Amy declared, ignoring his wisecrack. "Know why a Blackfoot would never kill a hibernating bear?''

He shook his head. "No—but I'm sure you'll tell me.''

"It was because of the Great Medicine Grizzly, a creature who watched over the tribe and saved them from their enemies. According to Blackfoot lore, the animal made a pact with the Indians, promising to help them, even fight for them, on the condition that they would never kill a brother bear that had holed up for the winter.''

"Didn't they also believe that owls were evil spirits?''

"That was because they didn't like things that killed in darkness," she replied. "They had a saying—I can't remember it exactly. Something about 'their ways are evil, because they shun the sun and travel only by night.' ''

"Maybe Count Dracula was an owl.''

Her eyes flashed. "Go ahead, joke about it. But the Indians were a lot closer to nature than we are. Their beliefs were sacred to them.''

"Lots of people believe lots of things," said her brother. "Doesn't make them true.''

"All I know is that I feel kind of spooked when I get up here in the high country. Always have."

"And you've always had the wildest imagination in the family." Josh grinned at her. "Think that might have something to do with it?"

"No, I don't. The feeling I get up here is *real*. To me it is, anyway."

"Okay. Okay. Only don't expect me to share it."

"I just *asked,*" she said, a bit defensively. She squinted ahead at their father. "We've covered a lot of ground. Do you think we're still on the right trail?"

"We are," nodded Josh.

And as if to confirm this, Paul Ventry pulled up, dismounted, and knelt beside a section of thornbrush. He extracted a tuft of wool from the brush, nodding in satisfaction.

"They came through here," he said. "This is fresh. Color and grease show it hasn't been off the pelt more than twenty-four hours. From one of ours."

They spent the better part of the day tracking the strays, descending finally into a sheltered coulee. Sheep droppings littered the ground.

"Here's where they bedded down for the night," Josh said.

"Right," agreed the elder Ventry. "With some luck, we should get a sight of 'em in the next hour or two."

He was correct. It was closing on sundown as they reined in their horses at the crest of a thick-grassed hill a few miles beyond the coulee. Paul Ventry carefully studied the terrain ahead through binoculars, then handed the field glasses to Josh. "Foot of the gulch," he said.

Josh adjusted the glasses, nodding. "Looks like a pile-up."

"That's what it looks like," said Paul Ventry, urging his horse forward. "Damn!"

It took them another half hour to reach the mouth of the narrow gulch in the heavily timbered area. The sky was swarming with magpies and crows; the scavenging birds set up a fierce chatter at the approach of the three riders.

A running lamb will follow its herd leader anywhere, and if that leader is unlucky enough to stumble into a ground hole, breaking stride, the herd will pile up behind him in the same depression, one over another, until most of them suffocate.

In this case, perhaps a half-dozen lambs had survived the pile-up, but they had been doubly unlucky since there was evidence that the survivors had been attacked and eaten by coyotes, their primary enemy.

It was a total loss.

"Sorry, Dad," said Josh. He put a hand on his father's shoulder.

"Waste. A damn waste," growled the older man. "Trouble with sheep is, they're *stupid*!" He suddenly grinned. "Or have I said that before?"

"Maybe a few thousand times," agreed Amy, returning his grin.

"We'll spend tonight at the camp," said Paul Ventry. "Ride back in the morning."

He looked sourly at the piled bodies of the dead lambs.

"Damn," he said.

# 3

AT THE BASE CAMP, HIGH IN THE LITTLE BELT Mountains, a roaring campfire held the night's cold at bay. With the evening meal over and done, and the cleaning up finished inside the shack, Paul Ventry used a stick from the fire to light his last pipe of the day. At the fire, Amy was warming her hands, the play of light accenting the burning red of her hair.

"Dad, there's something we need to talk about."

"What?" asked Ventry, finally getting his pipe going.

"It's about my future."

Ventry raised his eyes to her. "By God, you're in love! Is that it?"

"No," she said. "That isn't it." She hesitated. "I'm leaving Big Moccasin."

"Leaving? Why?"

"You *know* why. I'm not like Josh. I don't like living on a sheep ranch. I never have. Ranching's not in my blood. I don't belong here." She hesitated. "When Mom was alive . . . then it wasn't so bad. But since she's been gone . . ." Her voice trailed off.

"So now that you're all grown-up at twenty, you want to strike out on your own, right?" He stood up. "Hell! Can't say I haven't been expecting it." He drew in a breath. "But it still hurts just as much as I figured it would."

"I never want to hurt you, Dad."

"Had you on a horse before you could walk," said Ventry, eyes squinted against the fire's glow. "Taught you to toss a rope . . . use a rifle . . . handle sheep . . ." He turned to face her. "And all the time I knew you were hating it."

"I tried, Dad. You know how hard I tried. And as much as you'd like to see me get married, raise a corral full of kids, grow old and die as a rancher's wife, it just isn't going to happen. I won't let it happen. It's not what I want."

"Then what *do* you want?"

"A life away from here. A city life. Where I can meet a man who doesn't know that pregnant ewes need to be shorn at least two weeks before they lamb. And doesn't give a damn, for that matter." She looked intently at him. "I know a lot about sheep ranching—but I don't know much about *life.*"

"You could have gone east, to that university, the way you originally planned."

"There was too much to do here. You needed me. Mom needed me." Amy shook her head. "Maybe it was my fault—but I never left. Now I am. I have a train ticket to Cheyenne. And I've got a job lined up at Mountain Bell. Uncle Bob is there. He'll help me find a place to live."

"I see," said Ventry. His voice was soft, defeated.

She reached over to take his work-callused hand, pressing it firmly. "I'm sorry it has to be this way—but at least you've got Josh. He's everything you wanted in a son."

Ventry gathered her into his arms. "And you're everything that I wanted in a daughter."

She leaned into his chest. "But . . . I've let you down."

"Nonsense!" Paul Ventry declared. "I knew you'd never stay here after your mother passed on. Every week that's gone by since then I've waited for you to tell me what you're telling me now." He gave her a rough squeeze. "Dammit, girl, it's *all right*. I understand."

She put her arms around him, pressing her head tighter against his chest to hide the tears welling in her eyes.

Timmons, Edward Michael . . .

He killed his first human being in 1967, when he was twelve. Up to then he'd killed only animals, mostly stray dogs. He didn't write about any of his killings until he entered the state of Montana.

He gained a lot of attention in Montana. They called him the "Big Sky Strangler."

Montana made him famous.

# 4

FROM THE JOURNAL OF EDWARD TIMMONS:

*(Found by Sheriff John Longbow of Fergus County, Montana, in the ruins of Danvers General Store, Little Belt Mountains, November 10, 1991.)*

*Friday, September 7*

This is the first time of writing about myself. I never kept any journal from when I was younger. There's been a lot of pain in my life, especially when I was a kid, and I don't like to dwell on pain. It's negative, and I'm really a very positive person. You know, the *power* of positive thinking. Every thought we send out is an electrical impulse, like a tiny lightning bolt. And we have thousands of thoughts every day. Thousands! So here are all these electrical thoughts, lightning bolts of energy, going out into the world and if you are a negative person then you are sending out all this negative energy. It's like poison. It just screws up the whole atmosphere. It can ruin your life. That's why I believe in sending out positive thoughts. And that's also why I'm going to try and be positive in this journal, even about my faults and all. Hey, nobody's perfect.

The reason I decided to start putting down my life on paper is because I think these words can help me with my problem.

And it's pretty severe. The thing is, I keep on killing. It's a compulsion. Some people smoke—or eat too much candy—or drink too much. Now, I'm proud to say that I don't do any of those things. I used to smoke, starting back when I was in high school in Kansas, and it got to be a real habit (like the killing is), but I have a lot of willpower and when I heard all about how smoking ruins your lungs and does awful things to your heart and you get so you can't breathe (emphysema, it's called) and you get cancer and die, then I just quit. Cold turkey. I just said to myself, Eddie boy, you're screwing up your health with these "coffin nails" (what my Uncle Frank used to call them) and I never bought another pack of Kools again. (That's what I always smoked. I liked the menthol.) It's not cool to smoke Kools.

I'm not saying quitting was easy. I gained some weight and I went through a bad time for a while, nerves and all, but I stayed off cigarettes. The body is your temple. You don't foul it up. I'm proud of myself, about the smoking. It takes strength of character to do a thing like I did, but I've always been strong. In body and spirit.

I never got into drinking, the way Dad and Mom did. They both liked to get loaded and fight with each other. I mean, I think they really *liked* fighting and yelling because they did so much of it. Don't get me wrong—I'm no abused person. My Dad never hit me the way he did Mom. For one thing, when they began fighting, I got the hell out of the house. Sometimes I'd stay out all night and come back the next morning when they were both sober again.

They got along fine when they weren't drinking. And they both worked hard to bring me up. Mom worked in a beauty shop in Kansas City (and I'm talking about Kansas City, *Kansas,* not the other K.C. on the Missouri side of the river that most people think of as Kansas City).

Dad was in construction, working with the crews around town. I guess I hated him. That's a terrible thing to admit, but I know that when he died last year I didn't go to his funeral. Told Mom I had pneumonia. Phoned her from Chicago, where I worked at the time. I think she knew I was lying.

Mom could always read me like I was transparent. Hard

to hide things from her. When I killed my first stray dog she knew I'd done it right away. But I denied it. Never told her about any of my killings. Why get her all depressed?

She's still living in Kansas City, retired now, on Dad's insurance. He left her enough to get by on, and I phone her every month to make sure she's okay. I don't hate her at all. I mean, I think she's a very weak person, to take all that abuse from Dad and never leave, but she was always good to me and I appreciate that.

Mom is hard to get close to, because she hates hugging and kissing and all that kind of thing, and I didn't get those, but she was an okay Mom when she wasn't drinking.

I was her only child, and I often wondered what it would be like to have a brother or sister. When I was real little I used to pretend I had a brother my own age, and we'd have fights like Mom and Pop and I'd throw rocks at him. But he was out of my head and not really there, so the rocks never hit him. It was good, though, having someone to throw them at.

I called him Teddy and he was real to me. And he could be nasty. Sometimes he'd whisper in my ear, telling me to be bad (like when I set fires) and I'd do these bad things just to please Teddy.

I'm really rambling here on paper. I sure didn't expect to be writing down all this stuff about my family, but I suppose there's an awful lot inside my head after all these years that is just kind of spilling out into this journal. It must all be important or I wouldn't be putting it down, but I sure didn't start out tonight, writing here in the motel, to tell about my youth and all. I started writing to tell about the killings and how I plan to stop doing them like I did the cigarettes.

This morning, when I crossed the Bitterroot Range into Montana, and I killed the bald-headed guy who picked me up in his car, I told myself, hey, it's time to start putting down my thoughts about this compulsion of mine, to try and make some sense out of it and see it clear in my mind. All the other words just spilled out around the edges.

So let me get to the subject at hand.

Naturally, this bald-headed guy wasn't the first. And I know he won't be the last. (I smoked a lot of cigarettes before I was able to quit.) But killing him the way I did this morning, under this beautiful clean blue sky of Montana, made me really depressed. He was my first in three months, and I had kind of convinced myself that I was getting over the compulsion. Self-deception. We humans are real good at kidding ourselves.

I'd hitched across Idaho okay. Worked a burger joint for a month in Pocatello to get pocket money (among other things, I'm a good short-order fry cook). But it was important to get to Montana, so I quit and started hitching again.

There's an art to getting picked up on the road. Okay, not if you're some sweet-figured young thing in tight Levi's—but for a man it's a thing to do right or you'll never get anyone to stop. Just standing there with your thumb stuck out won't get you a ride.

First, you've got to look real friendly. You smile at every driver. You make eye contact. That's a strict rule in hitching, making eye contact. You have to look clean, too. Like with a shave and not shaggy hair and with no ugly stains on your clothes. I always carry at least one extra shirt and an extra pair of jeans in my strap bag, and I wash the dirty ones at a laundromat before I hit the road. If you look sullen and dirty, they'll just zip on past you like you're the invisible man. I always give them my best smile until my jaws ache. But you have to do these things.

Anyhow, just before dark, this old bald guy picks me up near the border in his Buick. Says he's headed for Missoula (where I am now), and I said great, I'd like to see Missoula. He had a classy new Buick, real nice, kind of orange-colored with wide seats. One of the big, roomy models. (When I was a kid I knew all the different cars, all their names, but now they look too much alike.)

The bald guy picked me up at night, which wasn't very smart, since I read that 80% of all hitchhikers have served time in prison, and it's bad enough picking them up in daylight. (I've never been in prison, by the way. What I do is considered wrong by society rules, I know, but not one police officer has ever arrested me for anything, not even for an unpaid parking ticket or jaywalking. My arrest record is spotless, and that's nothing to be ashamed of.)

Anyway, this guy stopped for me in his big chrome Buick and we crossed the Idaho border into Montana and got on Highway 10 and then onto Interstate 90 and it was so dark I couldn't see much of what the new country looked like, just the black highway unwinding in front of us. Minute I got into his car, this old guy started talking a blue streak, about how he was going to Missoula for some kind of farm equipment convention and how he planned to get some "kicks" at the hotel. Told me about last year when he had this red-haired prostitute up to his room and how she did all these kinky sexual things to satisfy him. Told me about looking down at all the freckles on her back as she did him. (Redheads have a lot of freckles.) Well, I didn't enjoy his dirty mouth. I don't happen to believe in pornography in any form, whether it's in a book or coming out of somebody's dirty mouth, so I just sat there, staring ahead at the highway, not saying anything back to him. (Mom brought me up never to talk dirty about the functions of the human body. You just don't discuss things like this.)

I could tell he didn't like my not joining in the conversation. I suppose he wanted me to tell him about the women I'd had and what we'd done together in an intimate fashion, but that was none of his business. So I was not feeling very friendly toward him, although I'm generally a good-natured sort. I just didn't like having to sit and listen to his filth.

I told him I had to take a leak and would he please pull off the Interstate so I could go. He makes some crude joke about the call of nature and we pull off onto a side road. Will this do? he asks me, and I tell him yes, it'll do just fine.

And that was when I strangled him.

He had a beefy neck and his eyes popped and I have to laugh when I think about it because he looked like a circus clown. All red and puffy. He thrashed around in the seat quite a bit but I didn't have any real problem killing him because I'm a very strong individual. I do pushups every night before I hit the sack to maintain muscle tone. It's a real shame the way most guys let thier muscles go to slack as they get older.

Anyway, after I got finished with Baldie, I drove his car deep into the boonies, siphoned gas from the tank, poured it all over everything, then set fire to the Buick with Baldie inside. Car burned like a torch. It lit up the ground, bathing the whole area in a kind of rosy glow, and it was real pretty to watch. Some things just have a kind of natural beauty about them no matter what the circumstances.

Then I hiked back to the Interstate and hitched on into Missoula.

# 5

_____

JOURNAL, continued:

THEY CALL MISSOULA THE "GARDEN CITY." THE town is set into an old lake bed, surrounded by the Montana Rockies, and it's a big industrial and tourist center. There's some fort near here where they built it due to the fact that the townspeople were afraid of the Flathead Indians. Back in the Old West days. Me, I never heard of that particular tribe, but there's lots of Indians I've never heard of.

I had a good steak dinner (medium, no onions) at this Overland Express Restaurant. Big tourist spot that's part of a place called the Mansion put up in the 1890s, shortly after the railroad came to town. Fancy windows and turrets and towers. Real Victorian. From where I sat in the restaurant there was a terrific view of the Missoula Valley and all these big tamarack trees lining Rattlesnake Creek, or at least that's what the waiter told me. Since it was dark, I couldn't see much of the terrific view.

I wasn't in such a good mood, so I didn't really enjoy the steak as much as I expected to. Somehow, it reminded me of the Buick guy's neck, beefy and red and all. The bread was good, though, I like whole grain wheat bread. Lot better for you than white. So I asked for that.

There was this girl in the restaurant, also eating alone like me. Pretty, but too thin. Real skinny arms and ankles. She kept looking over at me, kind of half-smiling sometimes. Now, I'm in my mid-thirties, and I've been called handsome by some, and I've got a great bod. All my muscles are well articulated. So she just locked onto me with her attention and I knew I could walk over and say hi and how'd you like to go somewhere for a drink and she'd up and go, neat as you please. I'd tell her I didn't have a car, that I'd hitched into town and she'd drive me in hers. When we got out away from the lights it would be real easy to kill her. That little neck of hers was thin as a twig. I could do her with just one hand, easy.

But I was still depressed over the bald-headed guy, and the whole point of writing all this stuff down is to help myself stop this lousy pattern of mine, this compulsion, and giving in to it here in Missoula so soon after doing the bald guy just didn't compute. I had to slack off, cut back on the killings so I could get my head straight and analyze this situation—so I just dropped my eyes to my plate and didn't return her smile. Just ignored her. And not long after that she left. And good luck to her.

I went to a late movie before going to the motel to sack out. I like horror movies. Not the grossout kind, where the teenagers get hung on meathooks and people get chopped up with axes. I mean the kind where you get a lot of mood and suspense and don't see too much blood. I'm no gore freak by any means.

I always sit in the fifth row back from the screen on the aisle. Close enough so that I can forget the audience and just kind of blend right into the screen and what's going on there. And I usually buy a box of Jujyfruits to go with the movie. Had a girl once who hated to see me eat them, because they stick to your teeth and you have to pry them loose with your fingernail. Said it made her sick to watch me doing it. But that was *her* hangup. Jujyfruits are my favorite.

The movie was called *Pit of Death* and it was all about this crazy farmer who dug this big pit in the back of his farm and then suspended a scythe over the pit on a rope so that whoever was down there would be tied up and waiting for the scythe to swing back and forth, lower and lower, until it cut them in half. It was based on some story by Edgar Allan

Poe, only updated to this modern farm where this family from the city came for a vacation. This crazy guy got each one into the pit and diced and sliced them. But what I liked, it was all done in good taste so you never really saw anybody actually get cut in half, just the suspense of them being down there in the pit, waiting for the blade. So it was a pretty good movie.

When I left and went to the motel (where I'm writing now) I thought how so many killers are just plain nutcases. I mean, in real life, not movies. (You have to separate the two.) Like that guy, in California, Charlie Manson, having these girl-friends of his go into Sharon Tate's house and butcher who-ever they could find in there like hogs in a slaughterhouse. Or that other California weirdo who chopped up maybe three dozen fruit pickers and buried them in some orchard. I think his name was Garcia, or some name like that. Wait . . . I remember! It was Corona, like the cigar. Or take that Speck guy that killed all those nurses on the same night, or the nut that climbed up in a tower in Texas and began shooting col-lege students.

Like I say, there are a lot of real freaks in the world these days who just make a terrible mess with their killings. Like John Gacy, in Chicago, who raped and abused all those teen-age boys and stuck their bodies into the dirt under his house. A true sexual pervert! And what about that Kemper guy from Atascadero who chopped up the coeds he killed and *ate* parts of their dead flesh. Now *that* is sick! Makes you want to puke.

And there was another joker (can't recall his name) who cut off this lady's head and used it for a dart board. A real primo nutcase.

Hey, I know that when someone reads these words they'll think, what about you, Eddie boy, you're a killer. What makes you so different? Well, for one thing, I don't just go around butchering every person I meet or going on some kind of blood rampage. In other words, I may have this need, or negative pattern, and I admit it is a problem, but I'm not some crazy man going around killing dozens of innocent peo-ple in berserk, disgusting ways.

Let's look at that word, innocent. First of all, *nobody* is innocent. (Except maybe babies and I don't strangle babies or kids. Never have. Never will.) We are born many times and live many lives. Dozens. Maybe hundreds or even thousands. And maybe on other planets, too, beyond this Earth. Maybe all over the universe. The actress Shirley Maclain (spelling??) has studied all this a lot more than I have and she makes a hell of a lot of sense. She says we carry our old sins around with us from all these other lives. We carry all this bad karma. So nobody who grows up into an adult is innocent. Nobody in this world, that's for sure!

There's another thing to consider: we all have to die, right? So when I strangle somebody (and I always pride myself on doing a good, quick job), it's not so terrible because that person is going to be dead anyway and it could well be that I have saved them from getting cancer or AIDS or having a whole series of painful heart attacks. Or from having a stroke. (Did you ever see pictures of somebody paralyzed all over so that only their eyes move?)

I'm not a violent person. Never have been. Maybe my Dad was, sure, toward Mom, but that is not relevant to my case. Truth is, I have never fired a gun in my life, not even a target pistol, and here I am 36 years of age! And I *hate* knives. A knife gives me the shivers, and I'd never use one on anybody.

When I kill, and this is a real important point to be made, I do it in a very clean fashion. In a pure way, with my hands. I make direct personal contact. It's like an act of communion between me and the one I strangle.

You take those two guys who butchered the Clutter family in Kansas. They're night and day away from me and my particular personality disorder. Which reminds me—I have to tell about meeting Truman Capote. (You pronounce it Ka-pote-tey.) He was the funny-looking little homosexual guy who wrote the book about those two sicko punks who slaughtered the Clutters. *In Cold Blood* it was called.

He went to the Clutters home town in Kansas and lived there for maybe three years and talked to everybody and finally met the two punks after the cops grabbed them and he fell in love with the one named Perry. Capote was homosexually drawn to this Perry and cried like a baby when they executed the guy. Claimed it was the worst day of his life, seeing this sicko punk put to death. It was all right there, plain as pudding, in the book, the way he loved this Perry.

Anyhow, I met Truman Capote the same year he died. Which was in 1984. (The year Capote died is what I mean.) I was back in Kansas seeing an uncle of mine (to try and borrow some money) and Capote was in town to sign copies of his latest book and pose for *Life* magazine. So I went to this bookshop where he was sitting at a table in the back, signing books like crazy. People were really making over him like he was the President come to town. Maybe that was because not a lot happens in Kansas, pretty dull most of the time, and him being there was major news.

He was real tiny, like a gnome, and he wore a white Panama hat. Never took it off. I heard him talking to people in this high squeaky kind of Mickey Mouse voice he had and it made me laugh to hear him. I laughed right there in the store. But I finally walked up to him and told him I'd read his *Cold Blood* book in a library which is why I hadn't bought a copy and that I don't read a whole lot of books but I'd read his about the Clutter killings. He asked me if I liked it, and I said yes, everything but the last part when he fell in love with this Perry creep, and that part made me kind of sick.

Well, he got all flushed and tight-lipped when I said this and he used the "f" word on me. "F" you, he said. I don't use words like the "f" word and you won't find any in this journal. So I was shocked at what he said—but I just shrugged my shoulders and walked out of there, out of that Kansas bookstore. I'd held my temper, but I don't like anybody using the "f" word on me, and that's a fact.

So that's how I met Truman Capote.

# 6

---

JOURNAL: Saturday, September 8

HAD A SCARY EXPERIENCE LAST NIGHT. WOKE UP and the whole motel was on fire, flames shooting up all around me, the ceiling above my bed burning and crackling with tongues of fire like dozens of wriggling yellow snakes. The fire was so real I jumped out of the bed, yelling, and woke up the couple in the next room. The guy pounded on the wall and told me to shut the hell up, that I was keeping him and his wife from sleeping.

I sat on the edge of the bed, sweating and shaking because the dream had been so real. I'm plenty scared of fire, but I've always been fascinated with it, starting when I was about ten years old and set the neighbor's trash barrel on fire one night. I got the matches from a shelf in the kitchen and used them to light a newspaper. Then I tossed it into the barrel and ran back in the house. The people next door called the fire department and I remember being real excited when the fire truck came down our street, siren going like crazy, with guys in big red hats jumping off it with hoses. It was all great to watch—and after that I set off three more fires over the next couple of years. One turned into what could of been serious. I set it at the edge of a corn field and the whole field burned. It was dry weather and that corn went up like a torch. An old farmer almost got trapped by the flames and I felt real bad about his coming so close to getting burned alive. But watching that fire eat across the field, like it had a hungry life of its own, the fire, well, that was exciting.

But the motel dream wasn't exciting, it was just frightening. Dreams sometimes spill over into waking time. I'll be having the dream, be really deep into it, and then I'll wake up and it will still go on. It takes me a while to figure out that I'm not still dreaming, like with this fire in the motel. It can be kind of intense, and I don't enjoy the feeling of being partly out of control and at the mercy of a nightmare.

Sometimes, back when I was a kid, I'd wake up from a dream and be so scared that I'd pee my pants. Mom would have to change the sheet, and she'd be real upset and when Pop found out I was doing this bed-wetting he said it was all her fault, that she was too easy on me and that I was a spoiled brat. Sometimes when he was extra mad he did threaten to belt me, but she'd get between us and he'd belt her instead. I was glad it wasn't me but it hurt to see Mom get smashed around. Once he knocked her through a window, so that the back of her head went through the glass and her scalp was lacerated. Lot of bleeding there. He said he was sorry, and took her to the emergency ward of our local hospital.

I stayed home and cried.

The first animal I ever killed was a brown squirrel. I was seven, and it was my birthday and Mom was mad at me for something I'd done (maybe wetting the bed) and wouldn't let me have a party or invite over any of my school friends. So I took my slingshot—which I'd made from a tree limb with a thick rubber band—and went out looking for something to shoot at. I found this fat brown squirrel in a tree, all hunched over and real intent on eating this nut he was holding, and I put a rock in my sling and let it fly. The rock hit him in the head and knocked him off the branch to the ground. He twitched a little, then died. I remember picking him up by his tail and spinning him around. He was real light. Hardly weighed anything.

Killing him gave me a feeling of power. Like I was a kind of Lord over the beasts and could let them live or die at my command. I killed three birds over the next couple of weeks and then I killed a skinny gray cat that hissed at me. When I was choking it the gray cat gave me a real deep scratch on my left shoulder. I told Mom I'd had a fall off my bike and she bandaged it. But it hurt a lot and I was real mad at the gray cat.

The next animal I killed was a stray dog.

I've killed lots of dogs since.

I've never been attracted to prostitutes. For one thing, you never know what kind of a disease they've got from some guy they've just intercoursed maybe an hour before you're with them. Even when they have medical checkups they can go right out that same day and intercourse some guy with AIDS and then you come along and stick it in there and get the same thing. They don't really care about making you feel good anyway, it's all just for the money so they can go out and buy some drugs or whatever. Most of them are strung out on drugs and they have haunted eyes. Think I'm lying? Go look into the face of a prostitute and you'll see those dead, haunted eyes, like the eyes of a zombie. Without feeling. Just like pieces of dead glass in their faces. I guess they get so sex is just nothing, they don't even feel what happens to them. I've never strangled a prostitute. I don't want to touch their skin.

The first one I ever went to was an accident. I was sixteen, in high school, and it was Saturday night and two of my buddies told me it was time I got laid. They knew I was inexperienced in terms of sex. So they drove me out to this roadhouse at the edge of the Missouri River at the Kansas border and took me inside and paid this prostitute to intercourse with me. They did a lot of sniggering and swearing and strutting around with her but she wasn't impressed. Just stuck out her hand for the money, in advance, then took me back to her room, which smelled like the window hadn't been open for a year in there, took down my pants, and rubbed me till I was hard and then got on top and rocked up and down till it was over. Took maybe ten minutes, the whole thing. My buddies were laughing and punching at me all the way back in the car, asking me how I liked it and I said it was great, but it wasn't great. It was just kind of sickening.

The woman was maybe forty and her skin was dry as parchment, and I could see needle marks on her arms. And she had those dead eyes they all have.

Believe me, it wasn't great.

# 7

JOURNAL: Sunday, September 9

I GOT INTO HELENA WITHOUT HITCHING. MY MONEY was holding out pretty good so I paid for a bus ticket into Helena and arrived at noon. It's the state capital, so I took me a tour of the place, trying to keep my mind free of the compulsion. It was crawling up my insides, like it had a life of its own, this need of mine. A lot stronger than wanting a cigarette, that's for sure. The guide was telling us that the dome of the capitol building is made of Montana copper with a statue of Justice at the top. I believe in Justice, in fair play and all, and I'm proud to be an American. In this country nobody tells you where to go, and you've got the freedom to take any road that strikes your fancy. In Russia you can't go anywhere without a pass. I'd go crackers confined to one town. I'm a rolling stone and I gather no moss. Want to keep on the move. Like that old song goes, Don't Fence Me In.

I've been restless all my life. Ran away from home when I was fourteen, and hitched all the way to Chicago before I ran out of money and couldn't get a job anywhere. So I went on back home. Kansas never thrilled me much. Flat and boring. No mountains. And I surely do love mountains. That's what I love most about Montana, the Rockies, with the trees climbing green on their sides right into the sky, miles of them in every direction. A state without mountains is like a pie without the crust. Just not finished somehow.

One of the things that interested me most about Helena was the Firetower. It was built in 1864 to spread the alarm in case a fire should start in one of the tents or wood cabins in Last Chance Gulch, and they called this tower The Guardian of the Gulch. Fires could spread fast in those days.

There's a scenic tour you can take through the Big Belt Mountains northeast of Helena, along unpaved roads. Spectacular views—and I would have enjoyed it a lot more if this young teenager with pink fuzz on his neck hadn't been sitting in the seat just ahead of me. The way the sun came slanting through the window of the tour bus kind of lit up these pink hairs on the kid's neck, and I could just imagine how it would feel to squeeze my fingers around that neck and crush those soft hairs flat against the skin . . . but I resisted. I worked to keep my concentration on the scenery.

When the tour ended and the kid got off and walked away, I never did get to see his face. Just the back of that soft pink neck walking out of my vision forever.

I congratulated myself for not following him.

Looks as if I'm making some real progress.

# 8

CRISTINE MITCHELL WAS NO LONGER COMFORTABLE in the mining tunnels below ground. Sometimes when she pressed her hand against the tunnel walls she imagined that she could feel the mountain's energy—its life. She could feel its vitality, as if she were pressing against the flesh of a gigantic animal.

As explosives supervisor for the Mitchell Mining Company (owned solely by her father, Blair Mitchell), she was unhappy; increasingly she felt that she was invading organic life as she performed her job.

At first, it had been exciting. As a fresh graduate of the New Mexico Institute of Mining and Technology, she had (thanks to nepotism) stepped into a dream job which was a professional challenge as well as a real adventure. Calculating the intensity of each blast, seeing that each charge was precisely placed, directing the men in preparing each explosion, the complexity of gold and silver mining had fully occupied her mind. Mining had become her entire life, taking the place of home, hobbies, and relationships.

Then she met Josh Ventry.

In many ways, she knew, they were polar opposites. Josh had never attended college; she was a college graduate and a licensed engineer. He was a sheep rancher; she was a professional miner. His home town was provincial Cameron, Montana; hers was sophisticated Tucson, Arizona, where the

"Western dude ranch" look was the end product of slickly designed resort architecture and expensive public relations advertising. Josh enjoyed braving Montana's below-freezing, snowbound winters; she loved Arizona's sun-blazed summers. ("I've always been a desert rat," she told him.) He'd only been out of Montana a few times in his life, on short trips to the surrounding states or to the Rockies just north of Montana's Canadian border. She'd been around the world twice.

But despite her misgivings about Montana, Cris had not been able to pass up her father's college graduation present: to become the explosives supervisor for the Mitchell mining operation here in the Little Belt. It was a professional coup other newly minted engineers would have killed for. To her, it was irrelevant that the invitation was extended solely because she was her father's only child. In business, she'd learned, you take your advantages where and when you can get them.

But Blair Mitchell was facing vehement opposition in north central Montana. Young adult Montanans had different ideas about mining than most of their parents and grandparents. In an earlier era, mining had been an important part of the regional economy. A network of largely abandoned rail tracks threaded the Little Belt, knitting together what had once been thriving mines. Boom towns had sprung up back then, dying as the mines played out, leaving dusty ghost towns in their wake. Slowly, the area began to revert to its natural wilderness state until, once again, it was sheep and cattle country.

Until recently, when Blair Mitchell convinced his financial backers that the old silver and gold deposits could be profitably mined anew. Mitchell purchased land and obtained mineral rights to large sections of the mountains, and he brought mining back to the Little Belt.

Against strong opposition. Protectors of Montana's natural environment lodged vigorous protests. Despite the concentrated efforts of local conservationists to obtain an injunction against opening and operating the mines, Blair Mitchell's corporation prevailed.

But Mitchell realized he had to gain local support. Without it, he would be constantly vulnerable to legal actions instituted by the conservationists. Therefore, he began his own aggressive public relations campaign aimed at winning the locals over to his side. He hired the best experts money could buy and developed a multifaceted plan.

Blair Mitchell became the biggest local booster in central Montana history.

Mitchell Mining sponsored several organizations at the Central Montana Exhibition and Fair, backed the newly inaugurated Lewistown Rodeo, and contributed heavily to every church and charitable organization in the county. The new library at Fergus Elementary School, the new auditorium at Big Moccasin Union High School and the obstetrics wing at Little Belt Hospital were all built compliments of the Mitchell Mining Company. Personally, Blair Mitchell bought two thousand boxes of Girl Scout cookies from local troops, contributing them to the Big Moccasin Food Bank. He bought a thousand boxes of peanut brittle to guarantee the success of the Lewistown Middle School campaign to buy musical instruments for the band. And he provided new football uniforms for the high school team.

Then there were the efforts of Mitchell Mining to make weekends in central Montana a little more exciting for the local population: semiannual free showings of such Disney classics as *Bambi* and *Cinderella* at the Judith Theater, an outdoor summer barbecue, with whole cows roasted on giant spits, and dances every month, with live music from local musicians and country-western groups imported from beyond Fergus County.

It was at a Mitchell Mining dance that Cris met Josh Ventry. She knew who he was; she'd seen him speaking out heatedly against her father at public hearings and had watched him leading antimining demonstrations in Lewistown. She was therefore amused when he came over to ask her for a dance.

"You wouldn't ask if you knew who I am," she said.

"I know who you are, and I'm still asking," Josh said, looking steadily into her eyes, a lopsided grin challenging her.

That dance was the beginning.

They had their first date the next night. Cris vividly recalled their conversation that evening. They were sitting at a corner table at Kwan's Family Chinese Smorgasbord in Lewistown, plates of chop suey, shrimp chow mein (the night's featured dish) and fried noodles in front of them.

"Cris, do you really believe your father is doing the right thing?"

"If I didn't, I wouldn't be working for him."

"Then you don't care about what mining does to the environment . . . to the *planet*?"

"Of course I care, but I think the situation has been twisted way out of proportion. Mining isn't new in the Little Belt. The area's full of abandoned mines."

"That's the key word—*abandoned*," said Josh. "Mining in this area was like a cancer that got cured. Now your father is bringing back the disease."

She shook her head. "I honestly don't see it that way. When you line yourself up with a bunch of fanatics and march down Main Street—"

He broke in angrily. "They're not fanatics! They're people who *care* about protecting the land. And it's not just for us, it's for everybody who comes after us. Our children. Our grandchildren. *Their* children and grandchildren. If we don't protect the land now, we're going to find that we don't have any left to protect in the future."

He paused, trying to find proper expression for his intense feelings. "Look, the decisions we make now are going to seriously affect the future of this planet. Take fast-food hamburgers, for example."

"Hamburgers?" She grinned at him. "You're going to mix mining with hamburgers? This ought to be good."

"Dammit, Cris, I'm serious."

"Okay, tell me the awful truth about hamburgers."

"A lot of the beef comes from cows raised in South America—where they're cutting down forests so they can clear grazing land. For the cattle. Trouble is, forests create the oxygen we breathe. So every time you order a fast-food hamburger, you contribute to the loss of oxygen in our atmosphere."

"Hey, whoa there, pard! I am *not* causing the destruction of the planet just because I eat an occasional burger!"

"Okay, I agree that the few *you* eat aren't going to cause more than a microscopic amount of oxygen loss, but if you add up all the millions of hamburgers that are sold—and consider the thousands of square miles of forests that have been cleared to create those hamburgers—we're looking at a potential future disaster."

She stared at him. "Wow! You *are* intense. So just how do all your millions of hamburgers tie in to mining the Little Belt?"

"Don't you *see*? It's the same kind of thing. This isn't the Old West, and mining now means a hell of a lot more than some old guy using a pickax and a washing pan. Modern techniques—the kind you practice—will result in catastrophic environmental change. And once that kind of damage is done, it can't be reversed."

Cris was astonished at his vehemence and passionate conviction. She was angry, but also touched. She'd never met a man before who cared so deeply about something outside himself. She didn't agree with him, not then, but she knew he was utterly sincere. Josh was by far the most interesting man she'd met in Montana.

Joe Kwan, owner of Lewistown's only Chinese restaurant, came over to the table, smiling as he interrupted their impassioned debate. He carried a tray with two dishes of pineapple sherbet and a plate of fortune cookies.

Cris looked—disbelieving—at her wristwatch.

"Josh, it's past closing. We've got to get out of here so the Kwans can go home."

"Sorry, Joe," Ventry said. "We just lost track of the time."

"No problem," he said affably. "Take as long as you want."

"Bring our check, and we're outta here," said Ventry.

Cris looked at her dessert dish. "I'm too full for the sherbet."

"Yeah, me too," nodded Josh. "But at least let's find out what's in our fortune cookies. Kind of fun, seeing what they say."

"I collect all the good ones," she declared. "I write the

date on the back, and then put them in an enameled tin box Dad gave me for my tenth birthday.''

''I'd like to see your collection, sometime,'' he said.

''Is that like coming up to see my etchings?'' she asked with a grin.

''Something like that, yeah.''

''Then why don't we take the fortune cookies to my place. We can open them there.''

That night they made love, coming together in a passion so intense it shocked them both.

The fire of that passion ignited a relationship that changed Cris Mitchell's life.

# 9

Over subsequent weeks a deep bond was established between them as Cris and Josh became emotionally interdependent. Inevitably, the beliefs of one began to influence the other. The younger Ventry's daily behavior was characterized by his deep affection for the land. As he rode with Cris on long trips into the mountains, showing her the areas he loved, her attitude began to change; no longer did she reflexively defend her father's position. She listened to Josh. She began to accompany him to conservationist meetings. And gradually she came to realize how vital it was that the region's natural environment be preserved.

Now, early on this chill morning in September, dressed in her white overalls, heavy mining boots and high-domed hard hat, waiting for the elevator to take her below ground to the tunnels, Cris had made a decision. She'd barely slept the previous night, torn between loyalty to her father and her growing sense of moral awareness. She loved her father and respected him for his sharp intelligence and habitual attainment of the goals he set for himself. But his present goal— what he was working to accomplish in the Little Belt—was now in direct conflict with her conscience.

"You ready, Ms. Mitchell?" Ed Hendricks, the shift foreman, gently nudged her shoulder, nodding toward the lift.

"Sorry, Ed." She smiled. "Guess I was daydreaming."

Hendricks looked at her oddly; in his experience, Cris

Mitchell didn't daydream. He'd never known anyone more dedicated to a job. That dedication, plus her proven expertise, had won the respect of every miner in the operation.

She stepped into the wire-caged lift, adjusting the light clipped to the front of her helmet. Hendricks followed, a big, square-bodied man, and the platform began to descend with a clanking rattle.

The trip down took less than two minutes. They jolted to a stop at the bottom of the deep shaft, stepping into a long rock tunnel, where a rail truck awaited them.

"Are the men out?" she asked Hendricks.

"All but Slater's crew. They're just finishing up in D tunnel. Should be done any time now."

"Well, let's make sure."

They sat down in the narrow iron rail truck, and Hendricks set it rolling. A series of overhead bulbs, spaced every ten feet, provided a dim illumination.

"Are the charges set in A?" asked Hendricks.

"They're supposed to be."

"Had a pretty bad rock fall last time we blasted there," said the big man.

"There won't be any trouble with this one," she told him. "The ceiling's been cleared."

Again, Cris experienced a strong sense of organic life pressing in around her. None of them belonged down here, slicing into the heart of this mountain. It was wrong, their being here now. Perhaps, in the earlier days of the last century, when the search for gold, silver and copper employed thousands, and a dozen boom towns provided economic life to the region, such an operation could be justified. But not anymore. Not in the 1990s.

Cris switched on her helmet light as they entered the branch tunnel.

The roaring sound of an air compressor assaulted them as the rail truck rolled into D. Combined with the earsplitting chatter of the tungsten drills, the noise was intense, all-enveloping. A miner who forgot ear plugs down here could end up deaf.

Four men were working the area just ahead, standing on a raised wooden platform, their heavy drills dancing against the tunnel wall. Sweat darkened their bodies as they sent down showers of stone to mound at the base of the scaffolding.

Conversation was impossible in this din. Hendricks climbed up to the platform, stepping directly into the miners' line of sight. He gestured, and they shut down their drills.

"You guys about finished?" asked the foreman.

The tallest of the four pushed up his face mask and nodded. "Just about. Another ten minutes and we'll be done here."

"Okay," said Hendricks. "We got that blast comin' up in A."

"We know," said the tall miner.

"Then I'll see you boys topside," said Hendricks.

The drilling resumed as the truck took Cris and the foreman down a branch rail.

In A tunnel, Cris double-checked each explosive charge set into the walls. The dynagel blasting powder she was using was a bit old-fashioned, but still effective. In many ways, mining had not changed much over the decades.

I could call for more powder, Cris thought. I could tell Hendricks that the charges as set won't be sufficient. I could arrange a blast that would close down the tunnel and delay the entire operation. They'd call it a mistake. Just a miscalculation on my part.

But what good would it do? It wouldn't stop the mining here; it wouldn't stop her father.

No, she told herself, just do your proper job this one final time and then quit.

That was the decision she'd made after a sleepless night. This would be her last job.

"Everything look okay?" asked Hendricks.

"Everything looks fine, Ed," she told him. "Let's head back."

The blast would go as planned. But, for her, it would mark the finish.

She would do no more to despoil the Little Belt.

# 10

JOSH FELT THE VIBRATION THROUGH HIS BODY. AS
if the mountain had shuddered. His horse, a strawberry roan,
skittered sideways, obviously startled and disturbed at the
deep-earth explosion.

"Easy, boy. Easy now, Red," he soothed, running his
hand along the animal's satiny neck. Red flared his nostrils
and nickered softly, then resumed the easy trot that carried
Josh toward the mining camp.

He dismounted in front of the main trailer, which served
as Mitchell Mining's corporate offices.

Blair Mitchell was working behind his desk when Josh,
ignoring Molly Grant's strident warning, pushed open the
executive office door and walked in.

"Well," said the big, silver-haired man. "You again."

"I tried to keep him out," said Mitchell's secretary.

"It's all right, Molly. I'll talk to Mr. Ventry."

She shot a cold glare at Josh, then left the office.

Blair Mitchell pushed aside the legal papers he'd been
working on, easing back in his desk chair. Beneath his carefully trimmed silver hair, the big man's face was ruddy, his
dark-shadowed eyes lined with sun wrinkles. His jaw was
wide and firm, giving his face a stubborn, unyielding look.
Indeed, Blair Mitchell was not a man to yield easily.

"You're a rude bastard," Mitchell said with a slight smile,

his eyes fixed on the younger man. "There was no need to storm in here."

"If I'd announced myself, I doubt you'd have been available," Josh said.

Mitchell nodded. "Maybe. I don't enjoy meeting with rabble rousers."

Josh grinned. "An interesting phrase. I don't think the good citizens of Fergus County would appreciate being referred to as 'rabble.' "

"The good citizens of Fergus County mind their own business," said Blair Mitchell. "I'm talking about the extremists."

"You call it extreme to care about the environment?"

"Obviously we don't agree on what's harmful to the environment." He rapped his pen sharply against the desk top and his voice became edged. "I have a business to run and I'm damned if I'll have a bunch of overzealous do-gooders telling me to shut it down."

"You're destroying the Little Belt, Mitchell. We'll *force* you to shut down."

"How?"

"Court injunction."

Mitchell smiled. "You tried that already. It didn't work."

"We'll try again," declared Josh. "And there are other ways to stop you."

"Such as?"

"We've prepared a petition asking the state legislature to pass a bill prohibiting mining in the Little Belt. We'll start getting signatures this weekend. Whoever comes to town Saturday or Sunday will be asked to sign. And after that, we'll go to every home in the six-county area, if we have to, asking for signatures. We'll go into the stores and churches. A month from now I guarantee we'll have most of the people in this region signed up."

"A waste of time," scoffed Mitchell.

"We'll see," Josh said. "But at least your daughter agrees with us. Cris knows that what you're doing here is wrong."

"That's a damn lie!"

"No, Daddy. I'm sorry—but Josh is right. I *do* agree with him."

Cris was standing in the doorway.

Mitchell swung toward her. "What the hell are you talking about?"

"He helped me see the truth," she said.

"And did he also help you into bed?" demanded her father.

"That's none of your business," she snapped, her eyes flashing. "My personal life has nothing to do with it."

"I think it has *everything* to do with it," Mitchell declared.

Cris glared at him. "As a major stockholder, I'm asking you to shut down the mining operation."

"Bullshit!" declared the big man, his face flushed with anger. "I gave you every share of that stock. It came from *me*."

"That doesn't change things," she said.

"When I die, you'll own the company, and you can shut it down then, if you're fool enough. But right now I hold the controlling interest. And I intend to continue to exert my legal right to mine the Little Belt."

"You won't even *consider* shutting down?" she asked.

"Damn right I won't!"

"Then I'm quitting. As of now."

Mitchell stared at her, angry and puzzled. "You mean that, don't you?"

"Yes."

"By God, when you act like this, I see your mother all over again."

"Maybe, Dad. But I think what you really see is *you*."

"Cris is speaking from her personal convictions, Mr. Mitchell," said Josh. "She's worked this out for herself."

"Fine, fine." Mitchell returned to his desk. "Then there's nothing more to say. Get out, both of you. I have work to do."

Cris stared at her father for a long moment.

Then she walked out of the office with Josh.

# 11

---

THEY MADE LOVE AGAIN THAT SAME AFTERNOON. IT was intense, consuming, a heated release.

In the slow, sensual afterglow of their shared passion they lay in close embrace, their naked bodies striped by late afternoon sunlight.

Suddenly, Cris giggled.

"What's so funny?"

"I was just thinking about those old movies," she said. "The kind they show on late night TV."

"What about 'em?"

"After making love, the man would always smoke a cigarette. You know, to relax afterwards." She looked at him. "Did men really do that?"

"Sure," said Josh. "Then, later, they died of lung cancer—but the movies never showed that. Cigarettes were big in Hollywood movies in those days. Until we all learned better."

"Nobody questioned things back then, did they?"

"People had the war to think about. Today, we're a lot more aware—of what we're doing to ourselves, and to the world we live in."

She rolled tight against him, pressing her full breasts to his chest. "I'm so glad you're in my life."

"Likewise," said Josh, kissing her ear.

"I needed someone like you to make me realize what my

father has been doing. He's poisoning the Little Belt the way a cigarette poisons the body.''

''It took a lot of courage for you to face up to him today—to say the things you did,'' declared Josh. ''I never expected you to quit.''

''How could I do anything else, believing what I do now?''

''My sister's a lot like you,'' he said. ''Amy faced up to Dad about leaving the ranch. She'll soon be heading for a new life in Cheyenne. Out on her own at twenty.''

''Good for her.''

''You're a lot alike, you and Sis. And I care a lot about you both.''

''You do? Really?'' Her lips were close to his, and the delicate scent of her hair excited him. ''Because I'm beginning to care a lot for you, Mr. Ventry.''

''Sure you're not just after my beautiful bod?'' he asked, grinning.

She rubbed her hand across his left buttock.

He pulled her close. ''I like the way your hair smells.''

''Special shampoo I order from France. Scent of roses.''

''Ummm.'' He cupped her right breast. ''I like everything about you.''

She giggled.

''I think we've talked enough for a while,'' he said.

''I think you're right.''

# 12

JOURNAL: Tuesday, September 11

I'M REALLY DISGUSTED FOR GIVING IN TO EMOTION the way I did today. There was this biker. A heavy-set character. Had long stringy reddish-blond hair with curls in it like waves on a beach, and fancy boots made out of dead snakes with caked mud on the soles. Wore patched brown Army pants with a Nazi cross on his jacket, and a big link chain padlocked around his waist. On the back of his sleeveless jacket, which was stiff with dirt, was this stitched insignia telling you the gang he belonged to: a horned demon with a pitchfork and the words, The Devil's Horsemen.

His hands were covered with matted red hair and looked like a pair of tarantulas, and his eyes were small and piggish and mean. He was stubble-bearded and had two front teeth missing. And instead of a helmet, he wore a wrinkled Army fatigue cap.

I was chowing down a burger in this little off-road cafe I'd hitched to between Helena and Butte. (I don't really enjoy eating burgers anymore because of what they feed the cattle, the kinds of chemicals and all they shoot into them, and I've been thinking about becoming a vegetarian, but that'll probably have to wait till I can figure out which vegetables are best to eat, the ones that are the most nutritious. I have to study on the subject first.) So I was eating this burger and not enjoying it much when the heavy-set biker comes stomping into the place, scowling and looking around for this girl-friend of his.

She was across the room on the far side of the counter from where I sat and the minute she saw him she popped off the stool and split for the door. But he caught her and slammed her head against the cigarette machine, yelling profanity. She twisted to get away and he gave her a kick that spilled her to the floor. Then he dragged her outside with nobody trying to stop him. Except for one waitress, and when she yelled something about calling a cop this biker gave her an icy glare and told her to mind her own f—— business and that if she called a cop he'd come back later and make her damn sorry she stuck her nose in. She backed off fast, looking pale and scared.

Through the greasy plate glass window I could see him haul-assing the girl into the parking lot. He pushed her toward his bike. One of those fat old Harleys with stitched-leather saddlebags. She climbed on behind him and they gunned away. He had an unmuffled exhaust and it sounded like a string of firecrackers going off as he peeled out of that gravel parking lot.

I forgot to describe his girlfriend. She was good-looking in a cheap kind of way. Really tight Levi's and a red tank top that made her boobs stick out and a washed-out denim jacket with The Devil's Horsemen insignia stitched in faded red satin thread on the back. Personally I didn't find her all that attractive, but I guess I'm just too particular about women. I've never had much to do with them for a variety of reasons I don't care to discuss on paper. Not that I'm what they call gay nowdays, or anything of that nature.

Well, this all happened in the morning, with the girl being knocked around and all, and I saw the biker again later in the afternoon. I was in Elk Park (didn't see any elks) and I'd just taken me a leak at a gas station, an Exxon, when I heard his cycle pulling in. There was no mistaking the sound of that firecracker exhaust. He was alone on the bike (don't know what happened to the girl in the red tank top) and he had a wine bottle in a paper sack. Got off the Harley, took himself a long swig from the bottle, then walked right past me on his way to the Mens.

I followed him inside. The place smelled pretty bad, like a lot of gas station men's rooms do, and there were wet, crumpled paper towels all over the floor. While the biker stood there with his pants unzipped I hit him from behind with a tire iron I'd picked up outside in the garage part of the station.

Like I have written, I am not a violent person, but this biker got me angry, treating that girl the way he had, and I just broke his skull. Cracked it like a rotten egg. He fell straight down and landed with his face in the wet paper towels.

When the bleeding stopped I knew he was dead.

I don't count this as a killing. This was an *execution*, eliminating a brutal criminal type, and therefore was truly justified. Sometimes you have to revert to the vigilante system like in the Old West days when they caught a horse thief and just strung him up to the nearest tree. Justice. Direct and simple.

The Exxon station guy was out by the front pumps around the far side, gassing a rusty Ford pickup, so I just climbed onto the Harley, kick-started it, and took off. Ditched it in a field an hour later.

Nobody even noticed me the whole time.

# 13

JOURNAL, continued:

SOMETIMES, SLEEPING HERE ALONE IN THESE strange Montana motel rooms, I have some weird dreams, so I figured I'd put some of them down in my journal to give insight into them.

Like the carnival dream. I'm a kid in the dream, maybe ten or eleven, and my Grandpa (on my Mom's side of the family) takes me to this carnival. It's one of the cheap road shows, run-down and seedy, with holes in the tents, and with most of the rides in bad shape, and with the Ferris wheel all rusted and unsafe-looking. The clowns look sad and the hoochy-kooch girls have sagging bellies and dead-fish eyes and wear lipstick like slashes of blood across their lips. They try to look sexy, but they're just pathetic. They make you sick.

Gramps says let's try some of the games and he buys two tickets for us to try the shooting gallery. I miss most of the painted tin ducks but Gramps hits every one, knocks them all down, and the guy in the booth, real fat and mean in a dirty white shirt all stained under the armpits, hands Gramps his prize. It's a live chicken. (In dreams, I guess you can win prizes like that.) Gramps takes the bird under his arm and we go into this water ride called the Tunnel of Terror. You get in this creaky dark green boat and it takes you around

47

corners in the dark where things jump out at you, and horns blare and you hear people screaming. (I hate being confined in dark places.)

Suddenly, in the middle of the ride, the boat stops dead still in the water and we're sitting there alone, me and Gramps. It's real quiet. Just the water lapping at the sides of the boat and the two of us breathing there in the dark. Gramps takes the chicken and holds it out in front of him. Then he starts to chuckle and next thing in the dream he's got his hands around the bird's neck and he strangles it. Then he hands me the dead chicken, with the head lolling loose. The chicken is wet and mushy, and I tell Gramps I don't want to hold it. Worms are coming out of it.

I throw the dead chicken into the water and when I turn back to Gramps his face is all lit in red, the Devil's face, and he has fur on his tongue and his eye sockets are empty, like the sockets in a skull. He puts his hands around my neck and begins to squeeze.

Good boy, he says, my good, good boy.

And I wake up.

Now what does a dream like this really mean?

Once I break this pattern of mine, and get the killings behind me for good, I've thought about where I'll settle down to start a new, quiet life. (Maybe work with flowers as a gardener; I'm good with flowers.) I think the best place for me would probably be the City of the Angels on the West Coast. Los Angeles. Yeah, I know there's smog out there, but smog doesn't bother me as much as cold and snow. I hate those little icicles inside your nose where the hairs get frozen. In Chicago once, I walked across a long metal bridge in a storm and the wind cut through me and it was snowing and I figured I'd die right there on that bridge before I got to the other side. So what's a little smog compared to freezing? In L.A. it never gets anywhere near as cold as places like Chicago and right here in Montana. It's fall here now, and it's nippy after the sun goes down, but I'll be gone before winter comes.

I'll just hitch on west.

*It prowls the night.*
*A stalker.*
*A hunter.*
*Seeking human prey.*

# 14

---

JOURNAL: Wednesday, September 12

    MY MOTHER ALWAYS READ THE BIBLE AND RE-
spected God, though I have never been a religious person
myself. I have my personal moral code, but don't follow any
Church or particular religious philosophy. But Mom loved the
Bible, kept it in a little drawer near her bed, and when I was
born she gave me the middle name of Michael. After Michael
the Archangel. She told me that I looked just like a little angel
the first time they put me in her arms at the hospital, and the
name just popped into her head. Edward Michael Timmons.
(The Edward was after my grandfather, on my father's side
of the family.) I was born in 1955, in early September, which
makes me a Virgo. But this astrologer once told me that because I was born in the evening, I have "Pisces rising,"
which means that sometimes I'm a typical Virgo and sometimes I'm just the opposite. (Pisces is the opposite sign of
Virgo, you see.) I dream a lot, I'm creative, and I also tend
to procrastinate, and the astrologer said these are all because
I've got the Pisces. But I'm also very clean, and I *hate* blood
or having anything to do with it, and I have real high stan-
dards about sex, and the astrologer said that's because I'm
mostly a Virgo. Many people scoff at astrology as a science,
but I know it's real. Leo people are almost always bossy and
aggressive. They think the world revolves around them. That's

because of their sign. Each sign has its traits, so people can scoff all they want, the facts speak for themselves.

I realize that what I am doing is rambling on paper so I won't have to write about my latest failure of intent. (I truly *intend* to stop killing.)

It was a woman this time. In her forties, but very well dressed and with nice subtle makeup and a good firm figure. She had a house outside the city limits of Butte, and asked me to go out there with her. Butte is a very ugly town, grimy and rusty-looking with hills that are too steep on land that has been eaten out by copper mining. Somebody told me that the mystery writer Dashiell Hammett had Butte in mind as a model when he wrote his *Red Harvest* book about an awful town that was filled with corruption. I don't know how corrupt Butte is these days, in terms of its city officials, but I wouldn't bet it has improved much.

I was in this shopping mall, just wandering around kind of window-dreaming (I like to hang out in malls) when this woman came out of a clothing store loaded with too many packages. She dropped one and I picked it up for her and she gave me a real warm smile. Would I mind helping her carry some of the packages to her car? I said, sure, glad to help, and we got all her stuff into this yellow Toyota in the parking area. I'm new in town, I told her, and I'm looking for some work, temporary, so I can get enough for a bus ride into Billings where my brother has a lumber business. He's going to hire me as soon as I get there.

Of course, this was all a lie. I don't even know why I asked this woman about getting work since I still had enough left in cash to hold me for a while, but I could feel the compulsion building up and she seemed like the one to satisfy it.

You can do some yard work for me, she said. The gardener has been sick and the weeds have taken over and I could use some help. I can pay you enough for your bus fare.

I nodded and said fine, I'd like to do that and she had me get in the yellow Toyota and off we went, headed out for her house on the edge of town.

It was a neat little place, one story, with an outside patio. Everything looked shiny and fresh-painted. Linda was a neat lady. (That was the name she asked me to call her.) She said she kept some work gloves in the garage and we went to get them and that's when I noticed she was kind of bumping my leg and touching at my shoulder. It was obvious she was physically attracted to me. Probably divorced or separated, or even a widow. I didn't ask. But she figured me for fair game, which made it a lot easier to follow the compulsion. I don't happen to appreciate whorish women.

The garage was real dim, with late afternoon sunlight seeping in through the door cracks and she looked kind of ghostly standing there with her white skin and pale clothing. Like she was already dead, which was ironic.

Would you like to kiss me? she asked, standing real close.

I could smell her perfume, a bit too strong for my taste, and I could see that her eyes were excited and shining. I didn't say anything. I just reached up to caress her neck, a soft white column there in the gloom, and she leaned her head against my hand like a cat will do, practically purring. I put the other hand on her neck. Goodbye Linda, I said, and squeezed, driving both of my thumbs into the hollow of her throat.

She was real shocked and did the usual thrashing and struggling, but like I've said, I'm strong, and that didn't bother me. Pretty soon she wasn't breathing anymore and I lowered her body to the floor of the garage. A shame the way the floor dirtied her. There was grease there from the Toyota and it smeared the whole back of her white dress. I have to laugh about the way I get over-concerned with little things. (That's a Virgo trait, by the way.)

In this case, the white dress really didn't matter, because she wouldn't be wearing it again.

# 15

AMY WAS SCHEDULED TO BOARD THE TRAIN AT King's Hill depot late Wednesday night, then transfer at Bitterroot for the run into Cheyenne.

She came downstairs, into the dark hallway, carrying her suitcase, wearing a new white pullover and a green Pendleton skirt with matching pumps. Not ranch clothes. City clothes. Purchased quietly on her last trip into town.

Josh was waiting, ready to drive her to King's Hill Pass.

"You look great, Sis," he said.

"I feel kinda shaky," she said. "Like I did the morning I had to make that speech at the Senior Assembly."

"Well," said Josh, "this is a special occasion, all right."

"It's scary," she declared, setting down her suitcase near the front door. The big house still smelled of lemon essence and warm beeswax, even though her mother was no longer around to clean and polish.

"I'll miss this place," she said, opening the round glass face of the tall, ornamented grandfather clock to move the minute hand forward. As usual, the clock was running slow.

"No, you won't," said Josh. "Not really. The truth is, you can't wait to light out on your own."

She laughed, punching him gently on the shoulder. "You were always able to read my mind."

Josh picked up her suitcase, ready to carry it outside to the Jeep, when his father's voice stopped him.

"Put that damn thing down," said Paul Ventry. "And come into the parlor, the two of you. I want to show you something."

"But, Dad," Amy protested, "the train—"

"Plenty of time," he declared. "Got at least a half hour extra. Plenty of time."

Amy and Josh exchanged a look. He put the suitcase by the front door and followed his sister into the parlor.

It was wide, with a stoutly beamed ceiling of dark wood. An overstuffed tassled Victorian sofa occupied its center, surrounded by heavy oak chairs and tables. Many of these pieces were family antiques, brought in by wagon at the turn of the century. A thick rug, sun-faded over the decades from scarlet to rose, covered the floor.

Paul Ventry nodded toward the sofa. Josh and Amy sat down. The elder Ventry reached behind one of the chairs, removed a tissue-wrapped box, handed it to Amy.

"A going-away present," he said. "Open it."

She smiled up at her father, stripping tissue from the box and lifting out the gift. A capacious cream-colored leather purse.

"Is it all right?" asked Paul Ventry. "I wasn't sure about the color."

"It's just terrific," she said, turning the purse in her hands. "The black one I have is way too small."

She stood up to give her father a kiss. "Thanks, Dad."

"There's a box of special stationery inside," said Ventry. "So you won't have any excuse not to write."

She smiled. "I'll write. And call, too. I'll be working for the phone company, remember?"

"What I can't figure is why you want to take a *train* to Cheyenne when you could fly there," said Josh.

"I like trains," she said. "The first long trip I ever took was on a train when I was six."

"To Kansas City to see your grandmother," said Paul Ventry.

He turned to Josh. "And as far as trains are concerned, young man, I'll have no unkind word said against them. It was trains that linked Montana to the rest of this country.

Amy's just lucky the passenger line still operates in this part
of the state. Freights are all that run most places these days.''

He sat down opposite his children, leaning forward, his
eyes softened by family memories. ''I ever tell you two that
your great-granddaddy, Newton Ventry, worked the U.P.
route and helped build the first transcontinental railroad? I've
got a photo somewhere showing ol' Newt standing next to
the president of the Union Pacific line at Promontory Point,
Utah, in 1869, when East met West by rail. What a day that
was! Hell, I've still got the gun Newt wore—Colt .45 with a
bone handle.''

Josh nodded. ''You showed it to us, Pop. I remember it.''

Indeed he did. His father kept the gun, complete with holster and bullets, on a shelf in the hall closet, carefully
wrapped in oilskin. The first time his father showed him the
old .45 he'd been a boy of ten, and he'd held it with awe.
Over the years Josh had gone to the closet and carefully ex-
amined the treasured gun several times.

''If people weren't in such an all-fired hurry to get places,
we'd have a whole lot more passenger trains still running,''
his father declared. ''And I say it's a damn shame they're
not.''

Now Josh and Amy were both standing. Josh tapped the
watch at his wrist. ''Gotta go. Solid piece of ground between
here and King's Hill Pass.''

Amy kissed her father, hugging him tightly. ''I'll call when
I get to Uncle Bob's,'' she promised.

Then she was gone.

Paul Ventry did not watch them drive away. He stood with
his back against the front door of the house, his eyes closed.

First Sarrie, now little Amy.

A double loss.

# 16

JOURNAL, continued:

TONIGHT I BOUGHT A PAPERBACK FROM ONE OF those Towne Book Stores where you always get a discount price. About the Boston Strangler. Let me tell you, he was one twisted dude. Each time he strangled a woman he was *really* strangling his own crippled daughter whose name was Judy DeSalvo. He was Albert. Also, he had sex with all these women, even the real old wrinkled ones, which is something I've never done and which very frankly turns my stomach. He used silk stockings to do the killing with, instead of his bare hands, and that's an impure way to do it and I have no respect for someone who would use such a method. I just cannot identify with DeSalvo at all, despite what somebody might assume we have in common. I would say, in my opinion, he was most likely insane and despite my failings I'm a very rational person with a higher-than-average I.Q. (I know, because I took a test they had in *Cosmopolitan* magazine, and I really scored high. Surprised myself. Prior to this test—and it was long, over two full pages in the issue— I had considered myself as average, with your average mind, but the results of this test showed that I was far above what is called "the norm." An awful lot of people in this country today are not even literate, let alone above average, so I guess I've got a lot to be proud of in the brains department!)

Talking about this DeSalvo guy reminds me of those other stranglers, the ones from L.A.—Angelo Buono and the mustached one, Ken Bianchi. They were called the Hillside Stranglers. First of all, Buono was just a sick thug with no class who enjoyed giving pain to women. He's not worth discussing. Ken is another matter. The guy is real good-looking, and I saw a photo of him wearing a tux with a nice buttoned vest that made him look very sharp. But he's as crazy as a loon. I mean, when they put him through all these question and answer sessions his voice would change and he'd tell the cops that all the killings were done by "me, Steve." Like the three faces of Eve, that movie. Ken claimed to have this inner self, this "Steve" personality, who hated women and helped his sicko cousin Buono strangle them with rope. (Again, an impure act.) According to what I read about his case, Ken was killing his mother. These women were a symbol of her, and he hated his mother.

So there is just no way for me to place myself in the same league with these mentally twisted people. As this journal proves, I'm not trying to hide anything. I am being open and totally candid about the things I have done and I make no excuses. But I also think it is plain that I'm not some wacko who goes around torturing and raping corpses and all that sort of garbage.

Personally, I think that such people should be locked up for the rest of their lives without parole or sent to the gas chamber or hanged or whatever. There is no hope for such people.

For me, I honestly feel, there is much hope.

# 17

BEING IN A TRAIN IS LIKE BEING INSIDE A COCOON, thought Amy. You're here, and the rest of the world is out there, beyond the window, moving past you like images on a screen. There were the lights of small country depots, the glimmer of waiting automobiles and trucks at a crossing; an occasional ranch, clusters of barns and corrals looming in the moonlight; the silver rush of water and the clatter of an iron bridge beneath the train's fast-moving wheels; the Little Belt Mountains shouldering darkly up from the edge of the plains, majestic in their quiet strength.

And me, here in the warm womb of the train, in the ticking rumble of a moving world, being transported to a new life. Amy took in a deep, slow breath, then leaned back in the cushioned coach seat, a smile playing at her lips. This was wonderful, a magic carpet hurrying her into the future. No more work boots and leather chaps or scratchy wool shirts. No more bawling lambs, or greasy camp food, or freezing hands inside heavy gloves. No more sheep dip or horse dung or branding irons or wool bales or fences to repair. No more saddle blisters or rope burns. No more sullen herders and stubborn horses who fought the bit, or coyotes, or frosted work on winter mornings.

She wouldn't miss any of it. Sure, there'd be some nostalgia later on; the harshness of ranch life would soften in her memory with the passage of time. But, here and now, in the clicking night world of the train, she was so *damn* glad to be leaving it all behind her like a bad dream.

She'd miss Josh and her dad, but that was okay; she'd stay in touch, seeing them when she could.

What she *really* missed was her mother. She fingered the gold locket at her throat; her mother's gift when she graduated from high school. She felt the engraved words: TO AMY, THE FINEST DAUGHTER IN THE WORLD, WITH LOVE. She'd wear it forever. The shock of her mother's awful death was stifling, insupportable. Amy had done a lot of crying, letting her grief spill out, not holding back like Josh and her father. But a lasting sadness remained, a deep ache in her heart. She knew it would take a long time for that ache to leave.

She put the past behind her, turning her thoughts toward Cheyenne, toward a new life among new people.

Cheyenne would offer a beginning, but she didn't expect to be there long. It wasn't a really *big* city; the men there were still rough-edged Westerners with a cowboy's idea of what a wife should be.

Seattle, that's where she would go in a year or so. Or San Francisco. Maybe even Los Angeles. Far away from the plains of central Montana where women were still expected to cook and clean and raise kids and serve their husbands in the rigid Old West tradition.

Her mother had fitted this mold. Sarah Ventry had been the ideal Montana wife, God rest her soul.

Not me, thought Amy. I'm a lousy cook, and I hate cleaning house, and screaming kids give me a headache. I want to travel, see the world, have a career that makes a difference. And I want a husband who likes to try good food in fine restaurants, a man who likes to talk about the important things happening in the world, who likes going to foreign movies and concerts and the theater.

In her entire life Amy hadn't been more than five hundred miles from Big Moccasin, and her foreign food explorations had been limited to the "Chinese" and "Mexican" restaurants in Lewistown. She had a strong suspicion that neither Pepe's West-Mex BBQ nor Kwan's Family Chinese Smorgasbord served food that was even remotely authentic. How could they? If they were authentic, nobody in Montana would eat what they offered.

The only foreign movies she'd seen were on cable TV and she knew that seeing them on a big screen, in a movie theater, would be a far different experience. The only plays she'd ever attended were performances by Big Moccasin Union High School students, mostly senior offerings of *Bye, Bye, Birdie, Oklahoma!*, and *The Pirates of Penzance*. She couldn't wait to see her first real, professional play, with real, professional actors. She'd go see whatever was on stage in the big city; she didn't care whether it was an ancient Greek tragedy or some modern avant-garde play with music that hurt your ears. She'd see *anything*. All she wanted was to be in a place where such things were possible.

She hadn't told her father about her ambitious plans. Let him get used to her being away from home. Cheyenne wasn't that far, yet it was far enough for her immediate purposes. He'd feel she was truly away from the ranch, living her own life, yet she'd still be—to him—comfortably in the West. A year from now, when she made the big jump to Seattle or San Francisco or Los Angeles, he'd be better able to accept her new role as a modern metropolitan woman.

God, it was all going to be so wonderful!

# 18

JOURNAL: Thursday, September 13

IN RETROSPECT, I'M NOT VERY HAPPY OVER WHAT happened in Butte, about what I did to Linda, but I can't be *too* hard on myself. It takes time to get over a habit, to break a long-standing pattern. I knew from the start that overcoming this compulsion wouldn't be like the way I was able to quit smoking, bang, cold turkey, no more cigarettes. I knew it would take longer, and so even though I'd like to believe I can just quit cold, it doesn't work that way.

But, granting all this, I am a strong-willed individual in the prime of health with a very positive attitude toward life so I know I can win out over my temporary personality disorder.

I just have to give myself a little more time and not be so impatient.

Time heals all.

Today I hitched a ride into Bozeman (it's between Butte and Billings) with a newlywed teenage couple who'd just bought this new custom Chevy and were real anxious to show it off. They talked about it all the way into town, about how it was like a space age car right out of an auto show and how they took just one look at it in the showroom and flipped. It was a neat car, that's for sure, and if the girl had been alone, without her new husband, I might have done something like taking it myself. I think I would have enjoyed driving it.

Bozeman is surrounded entirely by mountains and the lady at the Traveler's Rest Motel told me that if I liked fishing I could catch some prize trout from the rivers they have there. She also told me how the place got its name—from when John Bozeman led a wagon train over the Bozeman Pass, in 1864, to this valley and staked out the townsite. Which made me think that it would be nice to have a town named after me someday.

Timmonsville.

That isn't very likely, I realize. Still, it's a nice thought.

It was still early, so I went out for a look-see at the Museum of the Rockies they have here. A lot in the museum was interesting, relics and Indian stuff, but the one thing that really fascinated me was this skull of a tyrannosaurus (this is how you spell it because I got it right from the display card). Made me think of how no matter how strong and big you are, you can't beat death. These giant lizards ruled the earth zillions of years ago, and where are they today?

Nothing lasts forever. We all have to die. It's really no big deal.

I'm not afraid of death, and when it's my time, I'll accept it.

Dying is the most natural thing anybody can do.

# 19

WINTER WOULD SOON BE COMING TO THE LITTLE Belt. The days remained crisp and clear, warming by afternoon, but as the sun dipped closer to the western horizon, the temperature dropped rapidly, and the nights grew progressively colder. Hats were pulled low; bulky sheepskin coats and wool-lined gloves were worn against the cold. Ranch chores became oppressive once the sun had set.

Paul Ventry worked mechanically alongside Josh and the others; he found that Amy's leave-taking had created an enervating gap in his life, like a black hole in space, drawing energy and spirit from him.

He felt that the Good Days at the ranch were over. With both Sarrie and Amy gone, the place seemed sterile and empty. It needed a woman's touch, a woman's grace, to smooth the rough edges. No more of Sarrie's chocolate cakes; no more of the heaped bowls of buttered cheese popcorn that Amy loved to prepare. No more family discussions around a crackling hearth fire in the big living room.

Josh was gone, too, although not physically. He was a sheep rancher through and through, but there was a certain intensity to Josh lately that his father recognized. The older man knew Cris Mitchell by sight; everyone in town did. Josh hadn't properly introduced his father to her yet, but that was only a matter of time. If Paul Ventry was reading sign correctly (and he'd always been superior in his ability to read sign), Cris Mitchell was very likely to become his daughter-in-law. She and Josh would soon be starting their own life together. So although his son was still in the house, in truth he was nearly gone, too.

As he put on his plaid pajamas that night, Paul Ventry's thoughts were dark and troubled. There just wasn't a whole lot of reason to keep on living. Not that he would kill himself. He'd never do that, not unless he was terminally ill. In that case . . . maybe. He wasn't sure. But under normal circumstances, he knew that suicide was something he would never consider.

As he climbed into bed, sliding under the flannel sheets and Sarrie's prized goosedown comforter, he felt a closing, a darkening. He wasn't needed. Sarah, Amy, Josh. Nobody needed him anymore, or ever would again.

Ventry drifted off into sleep feeling empty and useless.

Paul was alone, standing bareheaded on the warped wooden platform of a small depot somewhere on the vast sweep of Montana prairie. Deep night. The collar of his fleece-lined coat was turned up against a black wind which cut at him in savage gusts. Above him, he could see giant clouds blown across the sky like a battalion of ghost ships. A pus-colored moon threw twisting shadows across the time-weathered platform. At the edge of the building, a faded sign creaked and moaned in the wind: SKULLTOWN.

The depot itself was long-abandoned, its paint-blistered doors boarded over with rust-red nails driven into the wood like dark bloodstains.

A passenger train waited, motionless on cold steel tracks, directly in front of the depot. A steamer, its high stack thrusting upward like an obscene finger.

It seemed dead. No steam issued from it, and its locomotive headlight gaped like a black eyesocket.

Ventry stood facing the train. The dream did not tell him how he had arrived there, or why.

The gusting wind whipped at his hair with angry intensity, cold darkness pressing around him like a shroud.

A movement at the corner of his eye.

Someone was waving to him from the far end of the train.

A pale hand, with beckoning fingers, ghost-white against the dark.

Someone.

Waving.

From the last coach, the train's only source of light. All of the other five passenger cars were dark and blind-windowed; only the last car glowed hazy yellow.

Ventry stepped off the platform and eased past the tall dead-metal bulk of the engine, his boots crunching in the cindered gravel.

He glanced up at the locomotive's high, double-windowed cabin; the glass was opaque, soot-colored.

Ventry moved steadily over the gravel roadbed toward the rear of the train, passing along the linked row of silent, light-less passenger coaches. The train bore no markings of any kind; it was a uniform, unbroken black.

When he reached the final coach, the figure had vanished. He peered upward at the windows. They were pale yellow from the interior illumination, but it was impossible to see any passengers who might be inside.

Then he caught a glimpse of movement within the coach.

Someone was there.

Someone who wanted him to enter.

Ventry mounted the metal steps. Reaching the platform, he tried the door. It opened under his touch, almost magically.

He entered the dimly lit passenger coach. A pair of ornate, scrolled brass lamps flanked the door. The guttering flame of their candles danced against the smoky cut glass, throwing twisted shadows down the long aisle ahead of him.

Ventry seemed to be alone in the silent night car. Along the length of the aisle, as it stretched away to darkness at the far end of the coach, the rows of green velvet seats were empty. Green brocade draped the windows, and the arched ceiling was carved with wooden faces. Their painted eyes looked down at Ventry, mocking him. He was a stranger to this inner train-world, an intruder on alien ground.

Yet *someone* wanted him here.

He had been summoned.

Then Ventry realized that he was *not* alone. A figure was standing, its back to him, at the far end of the aisle.

A figure dressed in black.

As he moved closer he saw that it was a woman.

With red hair.

She turned to face him, still small with distance.

"Amy!" cried Paul Ventry.

His daughter reached out to him, arms trembling.

"Daddy!" she cried. "I needed you—but you weren't here."

He began running toward her—as the aisle stretched before him. He ran faster, but the aisle seemed a mile long, a tunnel of pale light with his daughter waiting for him at the far end.

Running. Faster.

Until, finally, he reached her.

"What's wrong?" he asked. "Just tell me what's wrong and I'll help you."

She put her arms around him in a tight embrace, sobbing deeply. "It's too late, Daddy. You can't help me now."

She looked up at him, her skin very white in the dimness. Her red hair burned like blood in the candleglow.

"It's too late," she repeated softly, stepping away from him. "Too late."

And Amy began to *change*.

The flesh fell away from her face in gummy wet ribbons, revealing raw white bone. In the deep sockets of her skull her eyes rippled and dissolved, the fluid running down her cheeks. Her lips shriveled and melted as her teeth fell from her gums like rotted fruit.

Held in a thrall of horror, Ventry watched the ghastly transformation.

Then he screamed.

And awakened.

To the deep cold of a Montana night.

# 20

---

JOURNAL: Friday, September 14

FOR MOST OF LAST NIGHT I HAD A REAL RESTFUL sleep, but just before sunup, when the sky was going from black to gray, I had some bad dreams about killing my father, and I blame that Boston Strangler book. In the book it told about DeSalvo's father beating up his mother and knocking all her teeth out when he was seven. Now, my Pop belted Mom around, sure, but he never knocked a single one of her teeth out. DeSalvo hated his father for doing that and wanted to kill him. So that's why I figure I had this dream about killing Pop when the truth is he died a normal death. (I mean, his bad liver killed him, which is normal for an alcoholic.) What kind of a son would I be if I did a thing like killing my own father? He drank too much and he was a little rough, but I never hated him that much, and I sure never wanted to personally kill him. I mean, there were plenty of times when I just wanted to get away from him, and if he'd dropped dead right then and there I wouldn't have minded, but that's not the same thing as wanting to kill him myself.

I wish I'd never read that dumb book about Albert De-Salvo. Books like that put crazy things in your head at night. Today I ripped that book in half and threw it into the trash. People have to be careful about what they read.

* * *

I was checking out the malls here in Bozeman and at one of those Multi-Plex movie places where they have five or six movies all going at once, I went in and saw a Steve Martin comedy. Just to get that bad dream about killing Pop out of my head. Steve was his usual wacko self. (What a character! In real life I bet he's sad. All clowns are sad when they're not performing. Odd fact, but true.) In this comedy pic Steve played a trans-sexual (does it have a hyphen in it?) who was once a cheerleader in high school with ample breasts and a nice little behind on her in those tight satin pants they wear when they jump around at the games. There were some flashbacks to her showing her stuff at a football game. Anyhow, she has this sex change into this taxi driver who smokes big cigars and here the cheerleader's old boyfriend from high school shows up to marry her—except that now she's Steve Martin with a cigar and it was all pretty funny. Still, I have to admit I didn't think it was in very good taste. Why is everything you see in movies and television these days all sex, sex, sex? I'm no prude and I'm not any kind of Jesus freak or like that, but the plain truth is that dirt can get into your soul. It can erode your moral fiber. So who needs it? Frankly, I wish they'd do more Westerns.

I have always enjoyed a good Western. Take that one called *The Big Country* for just one example. A big, clean, outdoor story, full of action and without smutty sex. Gregory Peck was very dignified as the hero. Why don't they make more movies like that one? You just can't find good Westerns on the screen anymore. A good Western is like a tonic. Tones your system. I always feel great after seeing a good Western.

# 21

---

JOURNAL, continued:

I KILLED ANOTHER WOMAN TODAY. (YOU KNOW, people often call a woman a girl, but when a female is out of her teens you should call her a woman out of basic respect and common courtesy. This female I'm writing about had to be at least twenty-five, so she was without question a woman.)

She worked at one of those all-night places (this one was a Handi-Serve) and around midnight I bought a can of root beer (I like A&W best) and a Snickers bar from her.

She was kind of pinch-faced and her eyes were set too close together, but she was not what you'd call wholly unattractive. She wore a lot of cheap jewelry, rings and plastic bracelets and stuff, and she could have cut down on her eye shadow, but she was okay-looking.

It was her neck that attracted me. Kind of long and swanlike, without a single blemish, the kind of neck you see in oil paintings in a museum.

When her shift was over, I followed her to where she lived in this big apartment complex where there were dark paths and thick trees. Kind of a spooky place at night. Made me nervous, having to follow her in there, because I don't like being trapped in the dark.

When I was five years old, Pop locked me in a closet for a complete day and a night. I even had to relieve myself in there, in one corner, and the smell made me puke. Which of course made everything worse. I cried and banged on the door for hours, but it didn't matter. (I think Pop was out somewhere on a drunk and just forgot about me being in the closet.) Mom was away visiting her sister in Glendale, in California, that whole week, so she wasn't there to let me out. I got real, real hungry and got stomach cramps. A candy bar (yeah, a Snickers) which I'd had in my pocket was all I had to eat the whole time, and there was nothing to drink but my own pee and I didn't do that. (I've heard of people in the desert who drank their own pee, but the idea is revolting.) That time in the closet made me afraid of the dark, of being trapped and having blackness all around you. I can still feel that cold hardwood floor under my feet (I was barefoot, in my jammies) and I remember the clothes like hanging corpses swinging in the air as I banged and kicked at the door.

Anyhow, I followed this female into the dark area—and once she was inside her apartment I pressed the buzzer. A little slot opened and I could see her peering out at me. Wanted to know who I was, so I told her Sergeant Preston Hooker. (Got the last name from Bill Shatner's TV series which is now in reruns. I always like watching him on TV. He seems like someone I could really respect.) I flashed a fake wallet badge at her and she opened right up. I've noticed that people always open right up for the police. Inside, she asked to look at my I.D. again, but I just went to work on her, fast, pushing my thumbs into her throat. She made some funny, gargling sounds and then went limp as an old dishrag and I knew it was over.

It hadn't been difficult. I found myself grinning. I must tell you, in all honesty, that there's something humorous about how loose and floppy they get after I've done them. I guess that sounds cold, even cynical, but I don't mean it that way. It's just that living bodies are so different from dead ones and most people haven't experienced the difference. I'm trying to be honest with whoever reads this if anyone ever does.

I took the money this woman had in her purse (her name was Jeri-Ann Elston) and whatever cash I could find. She had some $20 bills stuck in a kitchen drawer (only a few) and I found a ladies wristwatch in the jewelry case on her dresser that looked like it might be worth something. But I left it there. I don't plan to risk trying to pawn a dead lady's wristwatch. Those things can be traced.

When I was ready to leave I was careful to turn out the lights because I don't happen to believe in wasting electricity. (After all, *somebody's* got to pay the bill.)

I took one last look at Jeri-Ann before I left; she was lying there in the living room, on her back, on top of a quite attractive blue and white throw rug. Her apartment was, for the most part, very tastefully decorated. Not overdone, like her makeup and jewelry. And the place was very orderly. I notice things like that. A lot of people don't. I've always prided myself on being an extremely perceptive individual.

I felt light and powerful going back to my motel. The way I always feel just after I've acted on the compulsion. As if something heavy and dense has been taken from me, a kind of dark mass that had weighed me down. Maybe that's how some women feel after their baby is delivered, or after you get rid of a tumor in a cancer operation.

The guilt will come later.

# 22

THE DEMONSTRATION HAD BEEN CAREFULLY planned. The marchers, more than a hundred men, women, and children, assembled just before noon at the western edge of Lewistown where banners and signs were distributed:

STOP MITCHELL MINING
NOW!

WE DEMAND A
SHUTDOWN!

SAVE THE LITTLE BELT!

PROTECT OUR
NATURAL ENVIRONMENT!

Josh Ventry was the group leader. He addressed the assembled citizens of Fergus County through a white metal bullhorn, his voice crackling above the crowd, braced against a cold northern wind, blowing down from Canada, which had begun at daybreak.

"Remember, no violence. We march four abreast, straight down Main to the Mitchell Building. Then we block the doors. When I give you the word, sit down in front of the entrance and link arms.'' Josh walked among the marchers as he continued his instructions.

"When the deputies come, they'll order us to disperse. Ignore them. If they arrest you, go limp. They'll have to carry you. Under no circumstances are you to challenge or resist authority.'' He raised his left arm high. "Are you ready?''

The crowd responded, stomping and yelling. They were ready.

"Then let's show Blair Mitchell we mean business!''

Flourishing the signs and banners, they began their march, breaking into cadenced song:

> *"Hut, two, three four,*
> *we won't take it anymore . . .*
> *We'll close Mitchell Mining down,*
> *we don't want them in our town!''*

The group moved east on Main Street—teenagers, a doctor and the town dentist, college students, merchants, two waitresses, three high school teachers, young mothers with babies on their shoulders, grizzled ranchers—an across-the-board mix of the Lewistown population, all fired with the same sense of outrage.

Sheriff John Longbow, a muscled six-footer whose high cheekbones and raven black hair testified to his Blackfoot Indian ancestry, stood quietly with two of his deputies under the marquee of the Judith Theater as the protesters passed them, shouting out their marching song.

Longbow waited until Josh Ventry appeared, then walked out to confront him.

"You joining us, Sheriff?'' asked Josh.

"You know damn well I'm not. But what I *am* doing is warning you,'' said the lawman. "I'll arrest anyone who attempts to block a legitimate business here in Lewistown. You've got the legal right to march and demonstrate, but that's all. You read me, son?''

"Loud and clear,'' said Josh. "You do what you have to, and we'll do what we have to. We're not backing down on this.''

Longbow shook his head. "I'm just sorry you figure you have to go this far."

"We'll go as far as Blair Mitchell forces us to go."

All along the route, the marchers were encouraged by on-lookers. People leaned from second-story windows to shout and wave; storekeepers stood in shop doorways, many of them grinning and gesturing thumbs-up.

It was clear to Josh Ventry that their case was a popular one.

But even Josh was surprised when Cris suddenly fell into step beside him.

"What are you doing here?" he asked.

"Same thing you're doing."

"I don't think your father's going to appreciate this."

"He'll be furious," she agreed.

"You don't mind?"

"Maybe he'll realize just how serious I am."

The marchers reached the Mitchell Building, a three-story structure of white fieldstone. Fluted white pillars flanked the entrance. Josh spoke crisply into the bullhorn.

"You all know what to do. So let's *do* it."

The protesters immediately moved to the tall gilt and glass entrance, sitting down directly in front of the doors in four tight lines, shoulder to shoulder, their arms linked.

Cris sat next to Josh in the first line, facing Main Street.

"At least we're out of the wind," she said.

Within moments, Sheriff Longbow's car had pulled to the curb, red lights flashing, while Fergus County's single police van parked behind him.

Longbow approached Josh, looming above him on the sidewalk. "Tell your people to disperse."

"I can't do that, Sheriff."

Longbow returned to his car, picked up a hand mike, and began broadcasting through his car's roof-mounted p.a. speakers.

"You are all in violation of state law and local ordinances," the sheriff told them. "You are blocking the entrance to a lawful business establishment. Move out, or each of you *will* be arrested. The choice is yours."

Nobody moved. Then the group began to chant: "Mitchell Mining has to go. We the people tell 'em so."

Longbow sighed. A dozen law officers (Fergus County's complete uniformed contingent) moved closer to the protesters.

"Okay," said Longbow. "Round 'em up."

"Go limp!" ordered Josh to the protesters. "Don't resist! Make them carry you."

Josh was the first to be arrested. He was picked up by two officers who taped his hands and dumped him into the back of the van.

When two of the other officers reached for Cris, the sheriff stepped forward, arm raised. "Not this one," he said. "She's Blair Mitchell's daughter."

Cris leaped to her feet, her hands fisted. "I *demand* to be arrested," she shouted. "I don't want any special treatment."

"Easy, Miss Mitchell—" began the sheriff.

"Easy, hell!" she exploded. "If you won't arrest me for protesting, then how about for assaulting a cop?"

And she kicked Longbow in the shin. He let out a yelp of pain, then pointed to the van. "Have it your way!"

An officer taped her wrists behind her, then put her in the van next to Josh.

He shook his head. "Your old man's gonna go apeshit over this."

"I know," she said with a broad smile. "Isn't it great?"

Fifty-three protesters had been arrested. Longbow had told his men to ignore mothers with small children, anyone younger than eighteen, the elderly, and those who had chronic health conditions. One advantage to living in a small town, he reflected, was that you *did* know everybody's business. He wasn't going to be responsible for arresting rancher Hugh Pritchett, for example. He'd never forgive himself if Hugh's lame ticker decided to stop working for good under the strain of a damn fool arrest like this.

The marchers, who called themselves CFCE (Citizens for a Clean Environment), were released under their own recognizance after two hours in custody—the time required to process the paperwork. Sheriff Longbow had no intention of adding unnecessarily to what this day was going to cost when the department's monthly expenses were toted up.

Before Josh was released, he was ushered into the sheriff's private office. Unlike the stark outer rooms of the jail, Sheriff Longbow's office reflected a deep love of Montana and Western life. Several historical paintings hung on the walls, interspersed with framed photos. Here were portraits of three earlier Fergus County sheriffs, rugged, tough-looking individuals. Over the door was a photo of Longbow posing with the governor of Montana and film star Robert Redford (who once made a movie in the Little Belt). There was also a photo of Longbow with President Jimmy Carter, who had come through the area on a campaign sweep. Longbow's desk lamp was a covered wagon and his desk pad was made of hand-tooled leather. A flat Papago basket held pens and pencils, and two small Cochiti pottery bowls were filled with paper clips. Longbow waved Josh to a heavy carved wood-and-leather chair in front of his desk.

"If I was a mind to, I could keep the whole damn lot of you locked up here until court convenes for its regular session Monday morning," he said. "But I'm not gonna do that. Not this time." The lawman scowled at young Ventry. "But I'm warning you, son. The *next* time you pull a fool stunt like this, I won't be so lenient. I'll let you cool your butt in a cell, and everybody else along with you. Got me?"

"You know what I think, Sheriff?" asked Josh. "I think you're in agreement with us. You don't like what Blair Mitchell is doing to these mountains any more than we do."

"It doesn't compute, son. As sheriff of Fergus County, I have official responsibilities. My personal opinions have nothing to do with my professional duties."

"Okay," Josh said. "I understand. But I still think—"

"You do your thinkin' back at your daddy's ranch," said Longbow. "And the next time you and these CFCE people want to protest, just stick to lawful marching. No more sit-ins."

"Thanks, Sheriff," said Josh as he shook the lawman's hand. "I hope we won't have to repeat our action."

"I hear you're gonna be sending around a petition asking

the state legislature to pass a bill against mining the Little Belt.''

''That's right,'' said Josh. ''We'll be sending it around starting today.''

''Well . . .'' And Longbow allowed himself to smile. ''Good luck with it.''

# 23

BLAIR MITCHELL'S LONG WHITE CADILLAC PULLED to the curb at the Fergus County jail as Cris and Josh Ventry exited.

Mitchell stepped out abruptly to confront them. He wore a cream-colored buckskin jacket and matching custom boots; his razor-trimmed silver hair gleamed in the afternoon sun. As Josh had predicted, he was furious.

"Are you completely out of your mind?" he demanded of his daughter. "How *dare* you behave like this? Marching with these fanatics, getting arrested, making a public disgrace of yourself. My *daughter*, for God's sake."

"Dad, I know you don't understand, but I'm doing what I have to do."

Blair swung toward Josh, his eyes narrowed. "You're responsible for this, goddammit, filling her head with your nonsense. She was an intelligent, sensible girl before she met you!"

Cris cut in with equal passion. "You might give me some credit for thinking on my own, Dad!"

Mitchell's face was rigid, and his tone was cold iron. "Next week, when I get back from Chicago, I'm going to draw up a new will, cutting you out completely. You give me no choice. God forbid that you should inherit Mitchell Mining."

"That's up to you, Dad," she told him. "If that's what

you think you have to do, go ahead. I intend to sell all my stock in the company. I don't want any part of it.''

Her father glared at her for a long moment without speaking. Then he said, ''You're a fool.'' He got back into the Cadillac and slammed the door.

Cris and Josh Ventry watched the long white car surge forward and vanish in the late afternoon traffic flow.

# 24

WHEN JOSH RETURNED TO THE RANCH AFTER THE encounter in Lewistown he was braced for a stern argument with his father. Paul Ventry had made it abundantly clear in the past that he had no patience with his son's involvement in CFCE. For the elder Ventry, politics and ranching didn't mix. Josh had taken time off from his duties to lead the Lewistown march, feeling justified; his attendance at the protest was vital. His father, he knew, would feel otherwise, and would make no bones about saying so.

Therefore, when Josh walked through the front door early that evening he expected to face a display of verbal fireworks. To his surprise, he found Paul Ventry sitting quietly in the den. The older man looked pale and shaken, as he had looked at his wife's funeral. An expression of deep pain lined his face.

The room was warmly furnished in maple and oak. Chintz curtains at the windows, and chintz covers on the sofa and chairs, expressed Sarah Ventry's traditional sense of interior decoration. Her milk glass vases and candle holders were proudly displayed on the mantel of the stone fireplace. There were several built-in bookshelves, containing volumes on sheep ranching, Americana, and Western history.

On the wall behind the desk: a massive oil painting of Sarah and Paul Ventry, on a high, grassy hill, mounted on their favorite horses, with the ranch spread below them under a fiercely blue, cloud-fleeced Montana sky. As a boy, Josh had marveled at that painting; it seemed majestic, awesome, larger than life. And the two proud-faced riders had seemed more godlike than human.

A postcard lay in the center of the polished oak desk.

Paul Ventry nodded toward it. "This came in today's mail."

Josh picked it up—a standard glossy tourist picture postcard of Montana. A mountain panorama under massive clouds with GREETINGS FROM THE BIG SKY COUNTRY! scrolled in red along the bottom.

Josh turned the card over. Postmarked Bitterroot.

> Dad,
> Please send me the white cable-knit
> sweater Grandma gave me last Christmas.
> I forgot it when I was packing. Mail
> it to me at Uncle Bob's. Thanks!
>> Love,
> > Amy
>
> P.S. The train for Billings just arrived.
> Guess what? It's an old black steamer.
> Didn't know they ran them anymore.
> I'm the only passenger, so I gotta rush.
> > X X X X X ! ! !
> > A.

Josh put the card back on the desk. "So? Amy forgot her sweater. No big deal. Just mail it to Uncle Bob."

"Damn the sweater. Amy's in danger," said Paul Ventry. He stared at the wall. "It has something to do with that steam train. I *saw* it in a dream. The same one she mentioned in the card."

"How could you dream about it when you didn't get the card until today?"

"Precognition," said Paul Ventry slowly. He looked at his son. "Remember—when Amy broke her foot up on Clear Creek ridge the summer she turned sixteen? I *knew* she was in trouble. I got kind of a 'flash,' and I rode up there and found her on the trail. The fall had spooked her horse and Amy was helpless with a broken foot. And I *knew*."

"Coincidence," said Josh. "You just had a hunch."

"I *knew*! Just like I know now," snapped Paul Ventry.

"Look, I'll phone Uncle Bob and let *him* tell you that Amy arrived safe and sound. Will that satisfy you?"

"She never got there," said the elder Ventry, softly. "You'll see."

Josh shrugged, turned to the phone and punched in the Wyoming number of Robert Ventry's law office in Cheyenne.

"Just a moment, Mr. Ventry," the secretary said after he'd identified himself. "I'll ring you through."

"Hello, Josh," said his uncle.

"Uncle Bob—"

"I was going to call you tonight. Has Amy's trip been postponed?" asked Robert Ventry.

"No, she left on schedule, just like she told you she would." Josh felt his hand tighten on the receiver.

"Well, she sure never got here," said his uncle. "And she didn't call."

Josh hesitated. Then, after a long moment, he said, quietly into the phone, "I'm sure everything's all right."

He was looking at his father's pain-etched face as he spoke the words.

"Call me soon as you hear from her," said his uncle.

"I will," said Josh. "Take care, Uncle Bob."

And he put down the phone.

Josh still refused to believe that anything had happened to his sister. "Amy's always been headstrong," he declared. "Did just the opposite of what people expected her to do. She changed her plans is all."

Paul Ventry shook his head. "She would have called. She knew we'd worry if she didn't."

"Maybe Amy doesn't want us to *know* where she is. Wants to get settled in, with a job and all, before she gets back in touch."

"She *had* a job waiting for her—in Cheyenne."

"Obviously she decided not to take it," said Josh. "Working for the phone company was never anything Amy wanted to do. It was just going to be a first step for her."

"She tried to contact me," said Paul Ventry in a numbed tone.

"When?"

"In the dream. It was Amy, trying to contact me. I just hope to Christ she was wrong . . . about what she said to me."

"What did she say?"

"That I couldn't help her. That it was too late."

And Paul Ventry lowered his head into his hands.

*The grind of teeth on bone.*

*A ripping, a savage tearing at crimsoned flesh. The violent separation of body parts.*

*The satisfaction of a kill.*

*Satiated.*

*Fulfilled.*

# 25

JOURNAL: Saturday, September 15

I'M NOT MAKING MUCH PROGRESS AGAINST THE COM-
pulsion, that's for sure. I promised myself that I'd break this
obsessive pattern, and what have I done? I've killed three
people since crossing the Montana border. (That scummy
biker would make it four, but I don't count him; he deserved
to die. As I have pointed out, his execution was a form of
basic justice.)

The papers and TV are beginning to pick up on the killings. But they haven't really connected them yet—the body
of the old man in the burned Buick, the dead woman in her
garage outside Butte, and now, last night, Jeri-Ann Elston,
from the Handi-Serve, that they found in her apartment.

When I got off the bus in Billings some people in the depot
were talking about the two strangled women, about the possibility that the same killer was responsible for both deaths.
An old lady grabbed my arm. She was shaking and her face
was dead white. Her hands were sharp-knuckled and bony,
like the claws of a bird. I live alone, she told me, and I'm
afraid to go home. Would you walk me to my door, young
man? It's only a couple of blocks, but I'm *so* afraid!

I told her surely, I'd walk with her, and that she had nothing to fear. She reminded me of pictures I'd seen of my
grandmother. On Pop's side of the family. She'd died the year

I was born, so I never got to know her. Mom's mother I saw just once, when I was ten. She was short and real thin and had glittery eyes; she was in some kind of institution and I never saw her again.

The old lady wanted me to come inside and have some cake and milk. She made me feel like a little kid. I told her no thanks, I had to be going. She clung to me with those bony fingers and I finally had to pry them loose. I don't want to die, she said softly. And I smiled at her. Nobody *wants* to, I told her. But it's just something we all have to do.

She was crying when I walked away. I didn't look back at her. You'd think I was her long-lost son leaving home. The old lady was a fool.

It was depressing.

Lot of history in this town, in Billings. Blackfoot and Crow country. Calamity Jane had a cabin here. (Unlike the way they show her in movies, she was ugly as mud.) Yellowstone Kelly and Buffalo Bill roamed this area. The Rimrocks keep the worst of the winter winds out, and summers are cool and sweet. At least that's what it says in the pamphlet I read.

I didn't stay in town long, not when I found out that the Custer Battlefield was just one and a half hours south, on Interstate 90. The site of the last great Indian victory in 1876, when George Armstrong Custer got his butt kicked. I'd read about it and seen hokey versions of it in the movies, and now I could experience the real thing for myself.

Every geographical site where any kind of violent action has taken place retains the ghost of that action. That's a scientific fact. The ground vibrations go right up through your feet into your brain. Which was just how it was when I got out of the tour bus at the Custer Battlefield.

I stood there and looked down the rolling short-grassed slope toward the Little Bighorn River. That's where all the Indians were camped when Custer showed up with his soldier boys. It was like poking a hornet's nest with a sharp stick; about ten zillion Sioux and Cheyenne warriors poured out of there and slaughtered the Seventh Cavalry to the last man. Way I see it, Custer was an idiot and got what he deserved.

I could feel the vibrations in the ground. It seemed to tremble under the hoofs of a thousand galloping horses, and I could hear the screams of the dead and dying inside my skull. Be great to be able to step into a Time Machine and go back there and see ole Custer get chopped down.

Death is always exciting.

There was a museum at the Battleground and that's where I met a tall, long-boned guy with a full beard (like Castro) who said his name was Thomas Sims. We got to talking about how dumb Custer was to think he could whip all those Indians with just a handful of men. He wanted to be the next President, I said. Figured that a big victory here at the Little Big Horn would put him in solid with the voters. This guy agreed with everything I said. We had some lunch together and he invited me back to his place which was maybe fifteen minutes away. He was a history writer from Austin, Texas who was doing a book on Custer; he'd rented this house close to the Battleground where he could work on his book. He'd written a lot of other history books, but I'd never heard of him. Like I admitted to him, I'm not much in the heavy reading department.

I told the bus driver I wasn't going back to Billings, so he wouldn't be looking for me when they pulled out. And then I went with Sims to his rented house.

It was cozy. Kind of a rough-hewn rambling place near some thick woods with a little stream trailing through them. And over the sound of the running water you could hear birds in the trees.

Turns out this Thomas Sims was homosexual. Which was a big shock to me. I just never suspected it. He didn't act that way or look feminine or anything, but when we got inside his place he put his hand on my leg, real gentle, and told me that he found me very appealing and hoped I wasn't offended by his frankness.

I said no, it was okay, but not to get any ideas because I wasn't like that. He kept his eyes on me (very intense dark brown, almost black, like some forest animals you see) and he spoke in this low, sensual voice about how a lot of men have never done anything gay in their lives but that it was no big thing and that if I would just relax I'd enjoy myself.

That's when I decided to kill him.

I don't like people who try to corrupt me. And that's what he was doing, trying to pervert me into something I wasn't and didn't want to become. He had his bearded, fleshy face close to mine and I could smell the Irish soap on him, the one with the strong scent to it, Irish Spring. Made me sick, smelling it.

I didn't want to dirty my hands on him, so I used an iron poker he had in the fireplace next to a wire mesh screen. I just grabbed the poker and began hitting him, real hard, and he fell back, screaming for me to stop and throwing up both arms to try and ward off the blows. But that didn't help him. I just broke his wrists with the poker. And kept hitting him until his mouth filled with blood.

And then it was over and I could still hear the birds singing.

# 26

JOURNAL, continued:

KILLING SIMS HAD ME WORRIED A LITTLE. I WASN'T feeling guilty, mind you, because *he* was the perverted one—not me—and he'd come on to me with the goal of my ultimate corruption. So killing him was a right and natural thing and not part of the compulsion. What worried me was that if they found his body I could be tagged for murder. The tour bus driver from Billings knew that I'd gone off with Sims, and he'd be sure to remember it if anybody asked him (like, for example, the police).

Better if they never found his body. Like he'd maybe just gotten tired of writing about Custer and disappeared. So I slung him over my shoulder (he was slender and I could handle him easy) and walked out into the woods, where the trees were thick, and buried him deep, below where the animals could get to. Using a shovel I'd taken from the house to dig his grave. The odds were against anybody ever finding him.

Before I put him under I took fifty dollars from his wallet. Back at the house I looked for more cash and found another two hundred dollars folded into a book on his desk. I guess he kept it there as emergency money. Well, he wouldn't need it now.

Actually, I rate this whole incident as an example of cosmic good fortune. When you're in tune with the cosmos, good fortune always comes your way. But you must learn to flow with the cosmic current, not swim against it. It's just a matter of keeping your mind and body in tune with the cosmic flow, allowing good things to manifest themselves in your life.

Ask yourself, how many people are open to the proper cosmic vibrations? The answer, sadly, is very few.

I was feeling a little tense so I took a long relaxing shower in his bathroom. I just let the water rush over me, stinging hot, easing the tension right out of my body.

Wearing Sims' robe, a big fluffy white job, I sat down by his fireplace to kind of cool out before I got dressed again. There was a newspaper on the table; it connected the two women I'd done—the one outside Butte and the one they found in Bozeman. Showed pictures of both of them and gave their names. Mrs. Linda Sutton was the lady in Butte, and of course the name of the one who kept her apartment so nice was Jeri-Ann Elston, just like I said. Both single. Linda was a widow. And both were more attractive in their news pictures than they had been in real life.

Anyhow, this news story suggested that the two murders might be connected, that the same killer might have done both and that the state of Montana might have a serial killer on the loose. Yet the police were quoted as saying that they had no evidence to indicate the two deaths were related.

Local police are stupid, plodding fellows lacking drive and imagination. I have never feared the police; it seems absurdly easy to outwit them. Most murders are solved only when someone offers information which leads to the killer. Random killings almost always go unsolved, because they lack a motive—unless the killer himself goes to the police to confess, and I would certainly never do anything that negative and self-destructive.

Of course, there's some luck to it.

Luck is a strange word to attach to my compulsion, but there's no question about the fact that I've been lucky when it comes to picking my victims (as they're called by the news media).

I have a way of making people *trust* me. I possess what I suppose you'd call an "innocent charm." Plus I have the ability to pick out people who respond to me. I never project hostility or anger. And I have kind eyes. (My Mom used to say I had the eyes of a lamb, and I guess it's true.)

Anyhow, what I do or don't do is nobody's damn business. I had a good laugh out of that dumb news story.

I needed to put some space between me and the dead writer, so I took his Ford pickup out to Highway 47 and drove on to Interstate 94, leaving the truck in the back parking lot of Al's Grocery in Bighorn. It was dark by then, so I stripped the plates; by the time the local cops traced the car to Sims, if they ever did, then I'd be well on my merry way. (And to prove he was dead, they'd *still* have to find his body.)

But wait a minute! When they *do* trace the car, I told myself, they'll start searching for the writer's body and they might have dogs that can sniff out a corpse in the woods behind his house and dig it up. Then, with the tour bus driver's description of me, I would be in some big trouble. Better to totally destroy the Ford pickup.

Acting on this decision, I drove it to the edge of a high cliff, got out, and gave the Ford a push over the edge. It fell like a huge boulder, banging along the rock face and exploding when it hit the bottom. Kind of fun to watch.

Nothing left of that Ford now but some fire-twisted metal.

# 27

BIGHORN WAS A SPOT OF NOTHING IN NOWHERE, SO I grabbed a bus into Miles City. Nothing much there either, but I didn't care. It was after midnight when the bus got in, and I just wanted to find a bed and sack out.

The lady at the Bull Train Hotel told me it was named after the wagon trains that used to haul supplies into Miles City from the end of the railroad line in the Dakota Territory back in 1880. I wasn't in any mood to listen to her gabble, but I tried to be polite. That's the least you can do with strangers who are trying to be nice to you.

The bed was lumpy and there was rust in the plumbing, but I slept like a baby in that hotel. For nine hours.

I woke up to one of those Montana skies that are so blue they seem unreal, like the backdrop on a stage. I sat there by the window, squinting at that intense blue sky, telling myself that what I'd done to Sims wasn't part of my personality problem.

But as you know by now, I'm a sensitive individual, and I kept feeling a twinge of guilt, despite all my reasons not to. Then I told myself, hey, Eddie, you're being negative again, sending out bad vibes into the atmosphere. *Stop it!*

That made me feel a lot better—getting back into a positive mode, a positive state of mind. Any one of us can fall into a pattern of negativity.

The trick is, to stay on top of things.

# 28

JOHN LONGBOW PULLED HIS BRONCO INTO THE gravel lot behind the sheriff's station, set the brake, reached across the seat for his brown Stetson, put it on, then got out, locking the door behind him.

All of these actions were instinctive; his mind was fully occupied with thoughts of Amy Ventry.

Longbow was baffled by Amy's disappearance. Her father was convinced that she was a victim of foul play—perhaps a kidnapping. But, again, there was no evidence to support such a conclusion. Could she have been the victim of a random killer—her body buried somewhere in the mountains? Or had she simply decided she didn't want her whereabouts known? If so, it made no sense for a girl like Amy to do that, Longbow decided. She was not one of those wild types who dye their hair purple and hang razor blades from their ears. No, sir, Amy was a loving, caring young lady who wouldn't cause her family undue worry. So maybe Paul Ventry was right, saying what he did over the phone, about his being *sure* Amy was in some kind of trouble—maybe even dead by now.

Ventry was due into town for a talk. One thing about being sheriff, Longbow reflected, was that you never managed to get a day off. Somehow, you always wound up working Sundays, too. Longbow checked his watch as he entered the red-brick building. Almost noon. A man like Ventry was always on time, and he said he'd be here by twelve.

Sure enough, when Longbow reached his office, Paul Ventry was waiting there for him, pacing the area like a restless cat.

"Howdy, Paul," said Longbow, extending his hand.

"Sheriff," nodded the rancher, with a firm handshake. "Hope I'm not keeping you from lunch."

"Lunch can wait," said the sheriff. "I got me a real busy day here, with all that paperwork from yesterday's demonstration to finish, but I can always make time for you, Paul. Depend on it."

He waved Ventry to a straight-backed chair and perched on the edge of his desk, reaching for his cigars.

"Mind if I smoke?" asked Longbow.

"Hell, no. I smoke a pipe myself."

Ventry looked at the floor-to-ceiling relief map of central Montana that dominated the room; sections of Fergus County were marked off in a variety of colors. An antique brass spittoon gleamed from the floor; it had originally belonged to the first territorial governor. A tall wooden hatrack held another of Longbow's brown Stetsons; near the door, a padlocked gun rack contained several weapons, including two Remington pump guns.

"That postcard I showed you from Amy," said Ventry. "The one she sent from Bitterroot."

"What about it?" Longbow reached into his cigar box, stripped the paper from his selection, clipped one end, and lit the cigar, drawing deeply.

"You told me she had to have been mistaken—about the steam train she mentioned."

"Right," said the sheriff. "They don't run steamers in this area anymore. Haven't for a helluva long time. Even the regular passenger trains are being phased out these days. People want to get places fast. Trains are too slow."

"Amy wouldn't make that kind of mistake," insisted Ventry. "She was a train buff, like me. She'd know a steam train right off."

"That's well and good, her being an expert on trains and

all—but no steamers run in Fergus County anymore. And that's a flat fact.''

The lawman puffed out a billow of cigar smoke as Ventry stood up to face him.

"I didn't tell you before, because I figured you'd think I was crazy."

"What didn't you tell me?"

"I *saw* the black steamer Amy described in her card."

"You saw it? Where?"

"In a dream the night before her postcard arrived. I had a nightmare about Amy being in trouble and needing me." He hesitated. "She was *on* the train."

"You mean in your dream she was," said Longbow.

The rancher nodded. "And I think the dream was Amy's way of telling me she needed help."

"Uh-huh," nodded the sheriff.

"I told Josh, but he didn't believe me—any more than you do."

"I believe you had a dream, Paul, but to say it came from Amy—"

"—is crazy?"

"I wouldn't go that far," declared Longbow. "It's just a case of you being worried about your daughter and trying to tie the dream to her being away."

"You don't think she's in trouble?"

"I have no way of knowing what happened to her, but I'd wager you'll be getting a call from her soon. Young girls are frisky. They like to kick up their heels."

"Explain the card," said Ventry coldly. "Why would Amy mention a black steamer?"

"It was late—after midnight. It gets real dark out there at Bitterroot. The train that arrived at the depot, maybe it *looked* like a steamer—what with the shadows and all. Amy was excited about her trip. She just made a mistake."

"Sheriff," said Ventry in an edged tone, "a steam train stopped at that station and my daughter got on it. And that's the last we've heard of her. She never arrived in Cheyenne."

Longbow crossed to the wall map, tapped a finger against the Little Belt area.

"You want me to search these mountains for a steamer, is that it?"

"Yes. That's what I want."

"I can't do that, Paul. For one thing, I don't have the deputies to spare, and for another . . ." He hesitated, looking steadily at the rancher. ". . . I don't go looking for ghosts."

"This is no ghost train," Ventry declared. "Dammit, John, I *know* that it exists."

"I'd need proof of that—more proof than a few scribbled lines on a postcard," said the sheriff.

Without another word, Paul Ventry got up and left the office.

# 29

JOURNAL, continued:

I HAD WHAT I GUESS YOU'D CALL A MEANINGFUL relationship in Miles City. With Cora. She was a waitress in a cafe near my hotel where I stopped in for breakfast. Hardly noticed her when she first took my order. Eggs over easy (so the yellows are not broken and smeary), sliced tomatoes instead of potatoes, wheat toast dry (butter is mostly fat), and some decaf. All we got's regular coffee, she told me, which was when I really looked at her for the first time. Cute. Kind of small-bodied, but with a full bosom and soft brown hair the color of mouse fur. And she didn't look cheap like most waitresses do. She had a little white plastic nameplate pinned to her blue uniform which said "Hi! I'm CORA."

Skip the coffee, I told her. Just bring me a large orange juice. She nodded and told me she didn't drink coffee with caffeine in it either, that it kept her awake at night. And she smiled at me.

Guess I was feeling lonely because her smile got to me. I mean, it was special, kind of a signal that she wanted to be friends. I smiled back.

Next thing you know we're outside the cafe together at the end of her afternoon shift. She asks me if I'd like to go someplace for a drink and I said sorry, I'm no drinker. Neither am I, she tells me, but this particular drink is great.

She took me to Happy Hobbits, a health food place in the next block. There was a country-type grocery store in front (lots of healthy foods in big bins) and a snack bar in the back. Trust me, she said, and ordered a sweet lassi for both of us. I'd never heard of a "sweet lassi" before, but it turned out to be real good. It was made with plain yogurt and water and ice and different flavorings all mixed up in a blender and I had to admit it was tasty. She said that it was a real popular drink in India, where a lot of people are vegetarians and eat very healthy food. She told me she was in the process of becoming a vegetarian. She didn't eat meat anymore (hadn't for over two years), but she still ate fish sometimes. So she couldn't really call herself a vegetarian *yet*. But she was working on it. That impressed me, because she was working on *her* problem of becoming a vegetarian just like I'm working on my problem with the compulsion. And she was into the proper care of the body, just like I am. So we had a lot in common.

I told Cora I take vitamins—a little plastic "varsity pak" that I swallow after dinner each day. There's a Special B Complex tablet, an A-D-E Supplement, a 1000-mg. C-Gram, a 400 IU E capsule, a Calcium-Magnesium Supplement, and an Iron-Copper Mineral Supplement. Then I told her that I also take some organic zinc and a bee pollen capsule, and that I chew three Super Papaya Enzyme tablets after every meal to aid my digestion.

We had a great talk about proper body care.

Cora is a kind of an odd name to be called these days and I asked her how she came by it.

When I was born, she told me, my Mom had just seen that Lana Turner picture *The Postman Always Rings Twice*. She liked Lana's name in the film, so she named me Cora, after the character.

Yeah, I saw it on the late show once, I told her, and it was pretty good. She and her boyfriend end up killing her husband.

That was the part I didn't like in the picture, Cora said. I mean, how could a person just kill a nice old man like that in cold blood? Her husband treated her very decently.

They wanted his property, she and her boyfriend, I explained.

They didn't have to kill him, she said.

Cora had kind of greenish cat eyes and she turned them on me like two spotlights. Could you kill somebody for a reason like that? she asked.

There are a lot of reasons to kill people, I told her.

That's a funny thing to say. She blinked. It's almost scary, the way you said that.

Hey, I'm just giving you a logical answer. You asked me a question and I gave you an honest, logical answer.

She relaxed. Okay, I see what you mean. But I still didn't like that part in the picture.

Lana Turner was a waitress in the story, just like you, I said. She smiled at this, and said how funny it was, her turning out to be a waitress. She'd dreamed of going to Hollywood to be a star, too, just like Lana had in the movie.

Cora shook her head sadly. But I never made it and here I am.

I'm glad you're here, I said. We were now sitting in her car on the driveway in front of her trailer, and the sun was down and she asked me in to watch some TV if I wanted to. I said sure.

Her trailer was cramped and full of clothes thrown all over and dirty dishes and stuff piled around. She apologized for the mess and said she'd been too busy to clean it up.

I was kind of put off at how the place looked, but her cat eyes and the way she moved her body, like she had snakes under her dress, got to me.

So we made it together in her trailer bed on a mattress hard as a brick. She was real active though, and I didn't mind the mattress. Her melony breasts had big nipples.

Did you enjoy that? she asked me.

Sure.

Then why didn't you come?

I guess I was nervous. You're the first woman I've been to bed with in a long time, I said.

That should have made you come all the more, she said, frowning at me, her head back against the pillow with the sheet over her breasts. Do you want me to suck you?

No, I said. Maybe I'd better go.

Why? Don't you want to watch some TV? I've got some carob walnut brownies I baked yesterday, and there's some nonfat milk in the fridge.

I *did* feel hungry. We'd been together for hours.

So we had the brownies and milk and watched an old Doris Day musical. It was dumb, but Doris is a great singer, and that makes up for a lot.

Did you know, Cora asked me during the commercial, that by the time they're through high school the average child has watched seventeen thousand hours of television?

No, I said.

And that the average child spends only eleven thousand hours in school during the same period?

I didn't know that, I told her.

If I ever have any kids, they're not going to waste their brains on thousands of hours of crummy television, she said. Do you have kids?

No, I told her. I never got married.

Why?

Never found the right woman. I'm a rover. I don't like to settle down. Guess I'll keep roving till I die.

That's an odd way to put it, she said. You have an odd way of putting things, Eddie. And she was frowning at me again.

I'm not your ordinary kind of guy, I said. I like to think of myself as special.

I could never marry a guy like you, she said.

That's okay, I told her. I won't be asking you to.

And we sat there in silence, watching the rest of the Doris Day movie.

Then I left and never saw Cora again.

But that night, I would say I'd had a meaningful relationship.

# 30

JOURNAL: Monday, September 17

I DECIDED IT WAS TIME TO SEE SOME OF THE NORTH-
ern part of the state, and I found a budget car rental agency
in Miles City that had a sister office with a dropoff at Wolf
Point. I could leave the car there when I hit town, so I said
fine and rented me a silver colored 1985 Honda Civic for the
trip north. Had to leave a deposit (lucky I found that money
in Sims' house) that they promised I'd get back at Wolf Point
when I turned in the Honda.

Montana has spectacular cloud formations, which is why
they call it the Big Sky Country, and that afternoon, after I'd
left 10 and was headed north on 253, just cruising along with
nothing much on my mind, I looked ahead and there was this
gigantic eagle in the sky. I mean, a huge cloud just above the
horizon that looked exactly like an eagle. Beak, outspread
wings, talons and the works. It got me to using my imagination. I thought, hey, what if a giant eagle swooped down
from the sky and just picked my car right off the road in its
claws and flew away with me inside to a real high mountain?

He drops the Honda Civic into a huge nest he's got up
there full of unhatched eagle eggs. Then he flies off to take
a crap or to piss or whatever. (By the way, I don't think crap
and piss are like the ''f'' word and I feel justified in using
them without any apology as working examples of the way

we talk today and not words of filth. Crap is okay, but s— —t is not. I will never write the word s— —t in this journal.)

Anyhow, here I am in the nest with the eagle gone. I open the door of the Honda and jump out, pushing aside one of the massive eagle eggs to reach the edge of the nest. I jump to the ground and start climbing down the mountain, being really careful not to slip. I'm feeling very worried about the eagle coming back before I can reach the bottom. Sure enough, here he comes, big as a 747, swooping down at me and giving out with a high-pitched scream that nearly splits my eardrums.

He sinks those sharp claws of his into the flesh of my shoulders and carries me back to the nest. For food. That's what I am. He's going to feed me to the little baby eagles when they bust out of these eggs. Their razored beaks will rip me apart!

Which is when I quit imagining about the eagle because it was making me nervous and affecting my driving.

I don't like to think about being eaten alive.

# 31

---

JOURNAL, continued:

MET A WEIRD CHARACTER ON THE WAY TO WOLF Point. I'd just turned onto Highway 13, at Redwater River, when the Honda's engine began to stutter, missing badly. Felt like I'd lost a cylinder. I pulled off the highway and something glittered ahead. The afternoon sun, hitting the window of a shack. I could see it through the trees. Maybe there was a phone there I could use to call the car rental office.

The shack had a kind of thrown-together look, and it turned out McGrath had built it himself. He was the fellow who lived there, alone, out here in the middle of nowhere, the one who was sitting on a wooden chair just outside the shack's front door as I drove into his yard. He had the chair tilted back and his boots up on a box. Had a patched, dust-colored sombrero slanted over one eye, and a black leather patch over the other. Had a thick, ragged beard streaked with white and he looked mean. A skinny-ribbed dog growled at me from his lap.

He didn't move as I got out of the Honda and walked over to him. My car's going out and I need to make a call, I told him. Wouldn't happen to have a phone in there?

No, I wouldn't. Don't have no damn phone. Never will. A phone is an instrument of the Devil.

I just stared at him.

What's ailing your machine? Now he put the dog down, tipped the chair forward and walked over to the Honda. He spat heavily into the dirt an inch from the front bumper, shifting a wad of chewing tobacco from left cheek to right.

I don't know. The engine just started missing like crazy. I suppose it could be a fouled carburetor.

Open the hood and we'll have us a look-see.

I popped the hood and he leaned in, nodding. Ain't nothin' serious. Got you a loose ignition wire is all.

He fiddled around under the hood for a minute or two, then stepped back. That'll do 'er. She'll run fine now. Take my word.

Thanks. I appreciate your help. What do I owe you?

Some talk is all. It gets hellish lonely out here with nobody to jaw with. Just me an' the dog, an' you can't talk to a dog. You can, but they don't answer back. C'mon in. I got me some good whiskey.

I'm not a drinker, I told him.

Shot a' good whiskey never hurt nobody. He swung around to face me, scowling. Ain't sayin' no, are you?

I'll have a drink with you, I said.

And we stepped in. That's when he told me his name was McGrath and that he'd built this place himself. It was solid as a rock inside, and that figured because Montana can whip up some stiff winds in winter.

We sat down at a rough wooden table and he poured us two shots from a clouded bottle. Burned like fire going down.

McGrath smiled at the grimace I made. I could see he had two front teeth out. And I noticed the little finger of his left hand was missing. With his sombrero off he looked like a pirate.

You all alone out here? I asked.

Yeah-yah, he said. Had me an ugly wife for a while, but she up and died. No kids. No other kinfolk 'cept for a brother in Billings and he's an asshole. Ain't seen him in ten years and don't plan to in the next ten.

I looked around, shaking my head. I could never live out here by myself, I told him. I like to keep on the move. See new places, new people. I'd go nuts out here alone.

Hell, I usta be a city man myself, he told me. Had a profession and a little office of my own and wore city clothes and ate city food. I don't miss none of it.

What was your profession?

Sawbones. He held up his left hand. Took the finger off myself. It got infected and the sucker had to go. I was a medic in the war. Korea. That's where I lost the eye. Been wearin' a patch ever since. And I got a steel plate in my right leg to go with it from that damn war. You ever been in a war?

No. I don't like weapons. I could never use a gun in a war.

He spat out the open front door. Guess it takes all kinds, he said.

I asked him how he made enough to live on and he said it didn't take much, living the way he did. He had his war disability pension and a little money saved up. Enough.

That's when I got this crazy idea. About a cure for my compulsion.

I held my hands out, looking at them. The thumbs. That would do it. If he'd just remove both of my thumbs the way he'd removed the little finger on his hand I wouldn't ever be able to strangle anybody again. Without thumbs I'd be cured, and there would be no more killing.

You got a funny look to you, he said. How come you're starin' at your hands?

I almost told him. I came close to blurting it all out, everything, the full truth about my compulsion to kill, about the people I had strangled, about how much I wanted to stop doing what I felt compelled to do. All you have to do is cut off my thumbs, I almost said to him. Do that and I'm cured! But I didn't say it. For one thing, he could refuse. He could turn me in to the police. And why not? He was no friend; he had no reason to trust me. He might even fear my killing him to shut him up.

So I kept silent about what was in my mind.

Instead, I lied to him. My fingers ache, I said. Guess I was gripping the steering wheel too hard. Sometimes my fingers cramp up.

Could be a touch of rheumatism, he said. What you need is another shot of my best. That'll loosen you up.

Reluctantly, I agreed to a second shot. The whiskey didn't

burn as much going down this time, but it made me a little dizzy. I refused a third.

McGrath wanted to talk, so we jabbered, to use his word for it. He had some strong ideas on politics. Damned both the Republicans and the Democrats, said they were all corrupt, that we needed a clean sweep in government. He thought the country should form a new third party. He favored a strong-minded Constitutional Party to ''keep us on the straight and narrow.''

I let him jabber about all that, putting in a word or two along the way. I'm not into politics. Doesn't much matter to me who runs things back in Washington. I was thinking that there was nothing duller than a political speech, no matter who's making it.

One thing we agreed on, me and McGrath, was bodily health. And I'm grateful to him for what he told me about hemorrhoids and my prostate. Advised me to eat a handful of raw, unsalted almonds each day to take care of the hemorrhoids and a handful of raw pumpkin seeds to maintain a healthy prostate. Told me I could get them at a health food store; for him, he said, he ordered from a catalog and had a year's supply delivered every fall. Kept them in his root cellar so they'd stay cool and not get rancid. Advised me to keep mine in a refrigerator. He called it an ''ice box,'' though, and said that when he was growing up it had really *been* an ice box. Said his daily chore was to empty the pan where the dripping water went when the ice melted. Told me all about the man who used to come around in a horse-drawn wagon to put blocks of ice in all the ice boxes on the block. Said the man used to give him little pieces of chipped ice to suck on when the hot summer came, back when he was growing up in Nebraska.

I told him that I really appreciated his advice and I intended to follow up on it when I next come across a health food store. A person can never be too healthy. That's the philosophy I've always lived by, and I expect I'll still feel that way when I die.

McGrath asked me what I was doing in Montana and I said just passing through, seeing the country. Sure is beautiful, I said.

She's a bitch in winter, said McGrath. Cold enough to freeze the balls off a brass monkey. And he chortled. McGrath had a streak of vulgarity in him which I overlooked. After all, he was offering me his hospitality.

He did say one thing I thought was *really* obscene, and I hate to put it down here in this journal, but I'm trying to be honest and tell what happened and what McGrath said, so here it is:

Speakin' of beauty, he said, did you know that really beautiful ladies never have to take a s— —t? They're just too pretty to have to do somethin' that dirty. When they go to sleep at night, these tiny little elfs come marching into their bedroom and each elf carries a perfumed velvet sack. They jump up on the bed while this beautiful lady is sleeping and they just march right in through her pink asshole, collect what's in there, put it all into these tiny little perfumed sacks, then march on out—and she's clean as a whistle. He chortled loudly. Only *ugly* females have to s— —t, he said.

It was getting toward late afternoon and I wanted to get back on the road. McGrath was still chortling over his obscene elf story when I started the Honda. And he was right. It ran fine. Engine didn't miss a beat.

You come back this way, said McGrath, you be sure an' stop by, all right?

I said I'd do that. And I thanked him again for fixing the car. My pleasure, he said, and waved as I pulled out of his yard.

Strange one, McGrath. He could have cut off both my thumbs real easy. Cured me once and for all.

But I'd never ask him. Be a crazy thing to do, and I'm a rational man.

I'll just have to deal with my problems the best way I can.

# 32

JOURNAL, continued:

WOLF POINT IS THE AGRICULTURAL CENTER OF northeast Montana. Maybe five thousand people in and around the main town. It's located along the Missouri River and the Badlands are just south. The Wolf Point Trading Post used to service the old river steamboats that ran along the Missouri; now the building is used as a souvenir shop. All this was before the Great Northern Railroad pushed through to put the riverboats out of business. You can't ever discount the power of trains in this big country of ours. Maybe passenger service isn't what it used to be, but the trains still roll through Montana and the sound of those clicking wheels is music to my ears.

Guess I haven't put down anything in this journal about how much I loved trains as a kid. I'd go down by the tracks along the Kansas flats and just stretch out there on the ground, on my stomach, with my chin propped in my fist, real close to the rails, while a train powered by, booming along like God's thunder, quivering the ground with its big wheels, filling my ears with the roar. I'd squeeze my eyes shut to avoid the cinders. I could feel my heart hammering in my chest with excitement. Sometimes I'd be there for most of the day, watching these trains rush past me like giant cannon shells.

I'd stand up to wave at the engineer and he'd wave back. I

used to wonder where all the trains were going and who was on them and I'd hear stories from some of the road bums that hung around the yards, about how they rode the rails to far towns and strange places. And they'd tell me about various adventures they'd had. I was about nine or ten, and I guess that was when the fever to move and keep on moving really hit me. Kansas seemed a lot more a place to get away from than a place to stay in.

When I was twelve and killed my first human—as opposed to animals—it was at the rail yards in Kansas City. I might as well write about it here, in this journal, because killing somebody at that age is not your normal thing, I realize. It was the beginning of the compulsion.

She was a kid, just like I was. A year older, thirteen. Named Vanette. And I never meant to kill her. We were chasing each other through the yards, jumping the tracks and hiding behind old rusted freight cars and playing around when I caught hold of her and we fell to the ground. She could see that I was excited, being this close to her, that I was sexually aroused, and she began to make fun of me. She stroked my crotch, giggling. When I begged her to let me take her dress off so I could see her naked she got mean and said she'd tell her parents and they'd have me arrested. I got scared and put my hands around her throat. She beat at me with her fists, but I just kept tightening my grip on her neck. And suddenly, I knew I was going to strangle her to death—like I'd done with the animals—and it gave me a terrific sense of power. The power to end a human life. Vanette got purple in the face and her eyes bugged and pretty soon she wasn't moving anymore. She peed her pants just as she died. (A lot of them do that.)

I left her there in the rail yard, and the next day the newspapers said that a tramp had killed her.

Nobody suspected me.

All that night I couldn't sleep. I just kept feeling the flutter of her throat muscles under my thumbs. I wasn't sorry I'd done it, I was glad. It proved that I had this special power. It made me dizzy, the rush of it. Like a drug.

After that it became a habit, a compulsion.

A lot worse than smoking.

*Lovers. A man and a woman.*

*Embracing in the night. Oblivious to the world. Lost in themselves.*

*It moves toward them, pulsing with energy, with hunger.*

*They are amazed to see it, but they have no reason to be afraid.*

*Yet.*

*It lures them closer. They reach out, touch it with tentative fingers.*

*It does nothing. It waits.*

*They move into its dark orbit. It acts, suddenly, violently.*

*They are swept into darkness.*

# 33

JOURNAL, continued:

UP TO NOW, I HAVEN'T WRITTEN ABOUT WHAT brought me to Montana. That's because I'm not here with any goal in mind; I just figured that it was time to see this part of the country. I'd been through the South and a lot of places back East, but I'd never been to the Big Sky Country and just decided to come here and see it.

What I just wrote is a lie.

It's hard to tell the whole truth and nothing but the truth in this journal. In real life you have to tell lies every now and then, just to get by, but I promised myself I wouldn't do that when I wrote things down. So just ignore all that stuff about my wanting to see Montana.

The reason I'm here is Kathleen.

She's a kind of psychic. Not a real gypsy kind that tells you what's in your future by looking into a crystal ball. Not that kind. No, Kathleen reads your future from your past. She regresses people—takes them back into their past lives and then puts together the pattern for what will happen next in this one.

Dennis was the one who put me onto Kathleen. He's a rover, too. No steady job, just likes to bum the country, seeing what he can see. Works at gas stations and fast-food joints, gets tired of the grind, splits for some open country.

A lot like me, Dennis is. (I don't know his last name. He never told me. But there's a lot about me he doesn't know, either. Like the compulsion. I'd never tell Dennis about that.)

Anyway, Dennis and me, we were gassing away at a burger joint in downtown Chicago when he told me he'd been regressed. I didn't even know what he was talking about.

You don't believe that this crappy life is the only one you've ever had, do you? Dennis asked me.

I said I'd never given much thought to past lives.

Hell, I was a sheriff in the Old West once, Dennis told me. And I was a British soldier before that. And, way back, I was a female whore with Julius Caesar. They call them groupies these days. Kathleen regressed me back into these other lives. And she only charges twenty bucks a life. She's not into it for the bread. She just wants to help people.

The ashtray in front of Dennis was filled with butts, like a lot of crushed white worms. He was a chain smoker, and still is. Up to four packs a day. I'd quit by then, and it made me sick, smelling all those half-dead cigarettes. But Dennis liked to smoke. Used to brag that smoking gave his body something to fight against. Keeps my cells active, he'd say.

I asked about Kathleen. Where could I get in touch with her? The idea of going back into my other lives, if I'd really *had* any, was a grabber. It fascinated me.

She's in Oak Park. You can get a bus out there. He scribbled her address and phone number for me. Call her first to make an appointment. She's usually booked a couple of weeks ahead.

When I called her number this kind of low, smoky voice answers. I tell her that Dennis suggested the call and when could I see her to be regressed? She set a date for the session and I took the bus over.

Her place was on the bottom floor of one of those old musty gingerbread wood-and-stained-glass Chicago mansions. The top floor had been converted into another apartment and a retired dentist lived there. At least, that's what she told me.

Kathleen Kelly was redhead Irish. Pale skin, big saucer-blue eyes, lots of freckles—and with the firm handshake of a man. She had on a shapeless black dress, like sackcloth, and

after I'd followed her inside she told me to take off my shoes
and leave them in the hall. That's when I noticed she was in
her stocking feet.

Shoes constrict the blood supply and confuse the magnetic
vibrations, she told me. I can't get a clear reading when shoes
are worn.

Her apartment was like being inside a kaleidoscope—
jammed with books and seashells and mirrors and painted
rocks and oil paintings and colored glass globes. In the middle of the room was a huge red velvet Victorian chair. Under
it was a huddled puff of white fur with slitted yellow eyes.

Her name is Shanti, said Kathleen. It means "peace" in
Sanskrit. Say hello to the gentleman, Shanti.

The cat hissed at me.

Kathleen scooped up the animal. I'll put her in the pantry.
She won't bother us there.

I picked a framed photo off the table—of Kathleen in a
white lace dress holding hands with a dark-haired, broad-
shouldered fellow wearing glasses. A wedding picture.

When she returned I asked, Do you live here with your
husband?

My husband is dead.

Sorry to hear that.

Don't be, she told me. Death is never a thing to be sorry
about. It is something to look forward to. Death allows us to
enter the next house in our ever-constant universal cosmic
journey.

I wondered if she'd be that bland about death with my
thumbs in her throat, but pushed the thought aside. Since I'd
asked to come here, it didn't seem nice to be thinking this
way.

Just stretch out on the couch, please. On your back.

Why do I have to do that?

Because this is how I conduct my regressions—with the
person lying down. It's much easier that way.

I stretched out on my back. She slotted a music tape into
a player, sat down cross-legged on a black velvet pillow next
to my head, then told me to close my eyes, which I did.

The music was kind of spooky, but soothing. I'd never
heard anything like it before.

It's New Age, she told me. Called "Ascension Into the Light." It will help you make the transition from present to past. Do you mind the incense?

No, it's okay, I told her. In fact, I liked the drifting scent. Smelled like jasmine, which reminded me of when I went through the South. I always liked the smell of jasmine, which is why I like the tea they serve in a lot of Chinese restaurants. If it's a good restaurant, with high-quality food, they nearly always have jasmine-flavored tea in the pot. If you take the lid off, you can see little jasmine flowers floating around in the water and smell their perfume. That always makes the meal special. So Kathleen's incense was soothing and made me feel right at home.

Her voice changed. It became deeper, and slower, and kind of musical. Now I will induce, deep within you, an aura of peace, she told me. I will be putting you into a light trance state, but on a conscious level you will be fully aware of what's happening to you. At any time you can stop the process, if you wish, by simply sitting up. So even though I will be guiding you through this experience, you yourself will always remain in control. Do you understand?

I said I did, keeping my eyes closed.

Allow my voice to guide you, she said.

She began to speak in a lilting flow, telling me how to relax the muscles in my toes, and then going through every part of my body up to the top of my head.

Then she told me to imagine that I was lying on my back in a small boat, under a beautiful blue sky, drifting endlessly down a wide stream. The sun is on the water and the day is very peaceful. She told me that my body was now totally relaxed and my mind was now open to the cosmic flow of life. My mind was now able to drift back . . . back . . . back . . . through time itself, into an earlier state of life.

It was like a dream, only I was awake. I knew I was on the couch and I could hear cars passing in the street outside and once I heard some children run by, laughing and bouncing a ball on the sidewalk, but it was still very dreamlike. I could feel myself drifting. I was very much in Kathleen's apartment, and I was in this dreamlike state, too. But both things were happening at the same time and it was like peacefully being in two places at once. It was a good feeling and I liked it.

You have reached a shore, she said, her voice soft and melodic. It is the shore that will lead you into one of your past lives. Now get out of the boat, she told me, and begin walking. Tell me what you see.

My eyes were still closed, but—in the dream—I could see a castle. With stone towers and a big drawbridge. I described it to her.

Walk over the bridge into the castle, she told me.

I did. I could hear the sound of my booted feet crossing the drawbridge, feel the vibrations as I walked on the wooden planks. *Boots?* I told her I was wearing boots.

What else are you wearing? How are you dressed?

In chain mail, I said. And I've got a sword and shield. And a helmet . . . with the visor up.

Is this *your* castle?

Well . . . they're opening the big iron door for me and somebody is calling me Your Majesty. Hey! I'm a king! And yeah, this *is* my castle. And I'm limping. I've been wounded in battle.

What battle? The Crusades? Did you fight in the Crusades?

No, the Crusades haven't happened yet. It's before. And I think I killed another king. In the Black Forest. It's a little hazy, but I feel proud, really. Like a great warrior. Only . . .

Only what?

I feel guilty, too. I'm the last one left of all my men. I killed this king and got away in a boat, but all my men were slaughtered in the forest. I survived—and I feel bad about all my men.

Do you have a wife? Is she there in the castle to greet you upon your return from battle?

No, she died. Of some plague. But I've got a daughter. She's beautiful. Fourteen years old. Long blonde hair. She's hugging me like crazy. Really glad to see me home safe.

All right. I want you to move ahead in this life. It's a year later now. Tell me what's happening.

Oh, boy. I—I'm in the bed . . . *my* bed . . . with my daughter, and we're doing it. Or, I guess you could say I'm doing it to her. I'm . . . seducing her.

Is she willing to have you seduce her? Or is it rape?

She . . . she's fighting me, hitting at me with her fists and scratching me, but I . . . I'm just going ahead.

Then you *are* raping her?

Yeah, I guess. Oh, someone's coming in . . . with a sword. It's my younger brother. He's trying to stop me. Now I've grabbed my own sword and I've . . . stabbed him. Killed him. He's lying across the bed and there's . . . a lot of blood. My daughter runs out, away from me.

Do you go after her?

Yes. She runs out of the castle, across the drawbridge, and I follow her. Into the forest where . . . oh, oh, this is horrible!

On the couch, I'm moaning and sweating. I can't open my eyes, and the dream I'm going through is so real. I *know* it's a dream, but it seems to be really happening to me. And I don't like it. Not at all.

What's going on now?

The dragon. There's a dragon who lives in the forest . . . next to the castle. A fire dragon. He's got my daughter and he's . . . eating her alive. I'm trying to save her, but my sword is no good against him. His . . . hide is like . . . like iron, and the blade . . . of my sword . . . breaks on it and . . . I'm helpless. I can feel the heat from his breath searing my face. My skin is burning. I'm on fire!

I sat up abruptly on the couch, my eyes popped wide. My heart was pounding and I could hardly get my breath.

Relax, Kathleen told me. I realize that you have tapped into a traumatic moment in your earlier life, but you must lie back and close your eyes and allow me to bring you out properly.

I did, and Kathleen counted backward from ten to zero, talking me back to normal consciousness, and I slowly opened my eyes again. This time I felt a lot better, but I still had the vision of being devoured by the fire dragon.

Look, I told her, all this is crazy. Even if I *did* believe that I once lived as a warrior king, there wasn't any dragon. That's fairy tale crap. Dragons don't exist . . . and they never did.

We can't be certain of that, she said. Also, it's possible

you were masking. What your mind symbolized as a dragon might have been something else entirely.

Masking? I said.

It means that you were substituting one thing for another on an unconscious level. It's a means of avoiding the *conscious* realization of a more terrible reality.

Oh, yeah? What could be more terrible than being eaten alive by a fire dragon? I asked her.

I don't know, she said flatly. I wasn't there. You were. I know only what you have told me.

So what does all this mean? I asked her. Does it have anything to do with my future?

All of our past lives affect our future, she told me. This particular past life of yours is undoubtedly important in your present life because it is the life you chose to remember. We always remember first the lives which are most important to us now. Your future in this present life depends on how you handle the karma from the older life.

I don't get you, I said.

I would assume, she said, that you've fallen into some sort of destructive pattern in your present life. Is this correct?

I nodded. Yeah . . . destructive. I didn't tell her just *how* destructive. None of her business.

The destructive pattern must be broken, she said. Or else you will be a victim of the karma you created for yourself in the past life.

I was still sitting on her couch, but she'd settled into the big red velvet chair in the center of the room. Kathleen's head was back, her eyes were closed, and her arms were bent at the elbow, her hands facing each other at chest level, the fingers spread wide. She looked a little like my Aunt Helen, who used to hold her hands that way when my mother would ask her to help wind balls of colored yarn for knitting.

I am receiving . . . vibrations. You are surrounded by waves of magnetism. These magnetic forces reflect your levels of consciousness at this time. Montana. There is something about Montana. What does Montana mean to you?

Nothing, I said. It's a state. I've never been there.

Her eyes stayed closed as she talked and her voice was flatter, less musical. But still soothing.

Montana, she said. That is the place where the pattern must be broken. That is where your karmic destiny is leading you. Go to Montana and stay there until the turbulence in your life has been overcome. Your karma will manifest itself in a proper conclusion in Montana.

Then she sat up straight in the chair, looking at me calmly. She extended a hand. That will be twenty dollars, she said.

I gave her two tens. The whole thing seemed like a fake to me and I figured I'd wasted my time and money. Yet there was something in what I'd "remembered" that shook me. It was a dream, I kept telling myself. But I knew it was real, too.

You're telling me to go to Montana, aren't you? I said.

I'm not telling you anything. I have simply reported to you what I received from reading your vibrational aura. You are free to ignore everything I've said. We always have free choice at every moment during our lifetimes.

Well, from reading this journal you know I didn't ignore what she said. That's why I'm here right now, traveling through Montana. Because of Kathleen Kelly.

And that's also why I'm so intent in breaking the pattern in my life here in this state. If she's right in what she told me, I've got to break the pattern *here* or suffer some kind of really bad karma. Each time I give in to the compulsion I'm closer to it. I guess it's plain that I'm taking what Kathleen Kelly said seriously. It would be easy to write her off as a nutcase, but I don't think she is. I think she got a psychic flash regarding me—and that I'd better do something about it.

But I have to take things one day at a time. I have to build up my strength and personal resolve to break this pattern.

Before it breaks me.

# 34

SHERIFF JOHN LONGBOW LIVED WITH HIS WIFE, RE-becca, and a sleepy orange cat named Marlon (after the film actor) in an upstairs rented apartment just a mile west of the center of Lewistown.

They did not live there by choice. For the past ten years, John and Becky had talked of building their own home in Fergus County—but that's all it had come to thus far: just talk. They'd saved up enough money, but the time never seemed right for a start on their own place. John wanted to supervise the construction personally, and—to him—there had never been enough time for the project.

"Maybe if we'd had kids, that would have *forced* you to find the time," Becky had told him. He agreed that maybe she was right, but why speculate on what couldn't be. Due to female problems, Becky had been unable to bear children, and she felt a continuing sense of guilt because of it. She knew John had wanted a son.

So the years went by, and the Longbows continued to live in the upstairs apartment in Lewistown.

Now, as he climbed the stairs, John Longbow was in a sour mood. He'd just finished another lengthy conversation with Ventry, and trying to present a logical argument to the veteran rancher was like talking to a stone wall.

The sheriff didn't look forward to fixing supper, but since

Becky's recent foot surgery, he'd been drafted as the family cook. *Somebody* had to feed them, and Marlon couldn't cook.

When Longbow opened the front door his wife was lying on the couch, her heavily bandaged right foot resting on a thick pillow in front of her as she watched a television soap opera on cable.

"How can you stand that crap?" he demanded. "It's about as real as a Mickey Mouse cartoon."

Becky shrugged, drawing the collar of her faded blue quilted robe closer around her thin neck. "What else can I do? I can't walk on this foot for another couple of weeks."

Becky was an angular woman with dark, arresting eyes and delicate, blue-veined hands.

"You could try reading a book," the sheriff told her. "Improve your mind."

She sighed. "We've gone over this endlessly, John. I don't *like* reading, I like watching TV. And my mind's fine just the way it is."

"Okay, okay," he sighed, racking his hat and unbuckling his gunbelt. "Guess I can't talk sense to *anybody* today."

"Meaning what?"

He sat down on the edge of the couch, next to her. The orange cat jumped into Longbow's lap and the lawman began stroking Marlon in his favorite spot, just behind the left ear. "Paul Ventry phoned me about his phantom train. He's ragging me about doing a mountain search for it, and I keep telling him that the damn thing exists only inside his head."

"You think Paul's going senile?" she asked.

"No, no. He's as sane as ever. It's just that he can't accept the fact that maybe his daughter needs some time alone. She may not want to contact *anybody* in the family. Young girls can get that way once they've got the bit in their teeth. But he can't let go of the idea that some harm has come to her—so he dreams up this steam train story to justify it."

"Then you think Amy's all right?"

"I'd bet my hat on it. She just wants to spread her wings a little. They'll hear from her." The orange cat was purring rhythmically in Longbow's lap.

"Could I ask you to do me a huge favor?"

"Foot rub, eh?"

She smiled. It softened the angular planes of her face. "If you can make Marlon so happy, then I figured . . ."

"Sure, hon." He lifted the cat to the overstuffed couch arm, then reached down to remove her slipper. His fingers began kneading the flesh of her left foot.

Becky put back her head, eyes closed. "Oh, that's lovely! You're wonderful!"

"That's me," he nodded. "King of the Fergus County foot rubbers."

They laughed together happily.

Outside, a train screamed in the night.

# 35

JOURNAL: Tuesday, September 18

HOW COME YOU ALWAYS DRAW SKULLS ON YOUR napkin? That's what a waitress asked me today in the cafe here in Fort Peck (where I went after leaving Wolf Point). I came here to see the dam and relax by the lake and kind of cool out, and I'd been in the cafe three times already and each time I doodled a skull on my napkin.

I just like skulls, I answered the waitress. No matter how beautiful or ugly your outer face is, I told her, this is how you end up looking after you're dead. Skulls are basic.

I'd hate to think I look like that, said the waitress.

You do, though, I said. That's what we *all* look like, underneath. Just raw bone and hollow sockets.

She moved away from me. Guess she figured me for a weirdo. I balled up the napkin and stuffed it in my shirt pocket. Didn't want to leave it behind for her to show around. The last thing I need is to call attention to myself. I should have kept my mouth shut about the skulls.

This Fort Peck area is a kind of game preserve. They've got just about every animal and bird you can name (native to Montana I mean), right here in the area. Even have some buffalo—a small herd they use to exhibit to people who've never seen a buffalo. I'd never seen a live buffalo before I came here, either. The most interesting fact about this area,

123

to me though, was that it was once the prowling ground of the flesh-eating king of dinosaurs, Tyrannosaurus Rex. He would have made a meal out of my waitress quick enough.

Leaving just her naked skull.

# 36

JOURNAL, continued:

I'M BACK IN REAL WHEAT COUNTRY, AND I DON'T
mean Kansas. I hitched up Highway 2 into Malta and this
place is noted for its wheat farms (as well as its cattle
ranches). And, again, the scenery takes your breath away.
The Little Rocky Mountains tower over the area and the Milk
River tumbles through here and it's all really something for
a flatlander like me to experience.

But I don't feel like writing more about Montana scenery.
That isn't what this journal is for. I have to write down what
I did here in Malta, about how my personality disorder man-
ifested itself just when I thought I was finally making some
good progress.

It started out by the old trail marker at the edge of town.
I was standing there reading about how Kid Curry robbed
the Great Northern at this spot in 1901 and blew open the
express car safe, then disappeared into the Little Rockies.

My grandfather knew Kid Curry, a soft voice said behind
me. He even helped him rob a bank once.

I turned to face a very attractive young woman in a modern
frontier outfit. She looked like a cowgirl in a TV commercial.
She was even wearing a Stetson tipped back so the sun could
shine on her face. It was a sweet face.

We never had any outlaws in my family, I said. (I didn't

125

tell her I'd always been fascinated by outlaws.) Outlaws just went out and took things into their own hands in those days, I said. They didn't let anybody tell them what to do.

She angled her head at me, a crooked little smile playing at her lips. Are you like that? she asked me. Do you just go out and do your own thing?

I don't much like authority, I said, if that's what you mean.

You're new here, huh?

Yeah, I nodded. Just hitched in today. I'm kind of drifting through the state.

Hungry?

Sure.

Come on, she said, and I'll take you to a terrific steak house. You like steak?

Sure.

I didn't tell her I'd been seriously thinking about becoming a vegetarian due to the methods used on cattle in the slaughterhouses plus all the bad chemicals in their food. I just climbed into her Mazda truck and we drove into the main part of town, to a place called The Wagon Train, which was in a log cabin kind of building and had pictures of covered wagons painted on all the walls.

We were talking, eating the sliced French bread, waiting for our steaks.

Guess you think I was trying to pick you up? She gave me her crooked smile.

No, I wasn't thinking that, I said. People in Montana are real friendly. I figured that's what you were being. Telling me about your grandfather and all.

Good, she said. I didn't want you to have the wrong impression. There was something about the intense way you were reading that trail sign. I suddenly got curious about you. My Dad runs the local paper and I guess I've inherited his nose for news.

I doubt that there's anything newsworthy about me, I said.

Maybe you've got a dark secret you'd like to share with our readers, she said. Everybody has a secret.

I almost said—as a joke—Well, I strangle people. Just to see the expression on her face. I didn't, of course. But it was a temptation.

If everybody has a secret, what's yours? I asked.

I like to pretend I'm Annie Oakley.

Who's that?

Don't you know anything about the Old West?

Some. I know about Billy the Kid and Calamity Jane. I like Westerns. Movies, I mean.

Well, they made a movie about Annie Oakley, she told me.

Guess I didn't see it.

Annie was one of the great trick-shot performers, she told me. She could knock little glass balls out of the air with a rifle at full gallop. Rode with the circus. Ever since I was a little girl, and Dad let me practice target shooting out behind the barn, I used to dream of becoming famous and joining a circus and having my own special trick-shot act. Sometimes, when I'm alone at the ranch, I just put on my buckskins and grab my target rifle and ride out just like Annie would have.

Are you a good shot?

Pretty good. I've won some contests. At the Phillips Country Fair last year in Dodson I won my first silver trophy. Not just in the women's division, either. I outshot all the men!

I don't like guns, I admitted.

She looked amazed. I thought all men liked guns, she said.

Well, I'm one who doesn't.

But you like Westerns . . .

Sure, but that's different. It's make-believe.

The steaks came and we ate in silence for awhile. They were really good, just like she said they would be. And the baked potatoes were good, too. Lots of restaurants get sloppy with their baked potatoes and when you get them, they're all overcooked and dried out, or undercooked and hard, and nobody seems to care. These baked potatoes were prepared just right, like somebody took pride in cooking them. When I finished I wiped my mouth and thanked her—because she insisted on paying for the meal. I asked *you*, she said, and that means I pay.

Are you going to write me up in your paper? I asked her. I can see the headline, I said. Gun-shy Kansas Pacifist Arrives in Malta.

That earned me another of her crooked grins. Is that where you're from? Kansas?

That's where.

I've never been to Kansas, she said.

You're not missing anything. It's pretty dull. All we have is wheat—and you've got enough of that around here.

Things were going along well and I was enjoying myself when a certain way she moved her neck made me tighten my lips and stare. There was a flutter of excitement in my stomach.

That's when I knew I had to kill her.

# 37

JOURNAL, continued:

WELL, IT'S OVER NOW AND NORMA'S DEAD.

Her last name was Jeans. Norma Jeans—like the first two names of Marilyn Monroe, if you leave the "s" off of Jeans. (Marilyn was Norma Jean Baker before she became Marilyn Monroe and didn't have blonde hair at all. She dyed it blonde later, but most people don't know that. And by the way, I think she was killed by the Kennedy faction for having affairs with Jack and Bobby and then maybe trying to blackmail the family, or they were afraid that she would, so somebody in their political circle—which was pretty large—just kind of took over and got rid of the problem. Bingo. Made it all look like suicide. I firmly believe this and I have studied the case.)

I left Norma's body in some deep brush down in a canyon. I could have buried her but it's always a lot of work, digging a grave, and I'm sure no one will ever come across her body so why exhaust myself? I don't like doing unnecessary work. The animals will finish her off. There won't be much left after they're done.

I took a bus out of Malta and then I sat there in the bus telling myself, Eddie, you are a weak, weak man, giving in to this thing the way you do. When are you going to straighten up and fly right? It's just a matter of willpower.

Norma was sweet and there was no reason she had to die except that she happened to meet me. And my two hands.

I looked down at them, in my lap, at the long, loose fingers with the neat nails (I always keep them filed and trimmed as part of my personal hygiene) and the wide thumbs with a little bump at each joint—and I thought that maybe they have a will of their own, and that maybe it's my *hands* that are to blame for all this. Maybe they made me strangle Norma Jeans. But I just shook my head and smiled. Crazy thinking. Not worthy of me. So I just put those kind of thoughts right out of my head. I was tired and highly stressed or I never would be thinking in this irrational fashion.

How long would I keep on doing these things? It was kind of disheartening. I wasn't making very solid progress on my decision to overcome the compulsion, and I just sat there in the bus, feeling blue. Like some guy in a country-western song.

The bus rolled on toward Shelby, a long run up U.S. 2 out of Malta, and I tried to doze, but I kept waking up again.

So I just sat there feeling weak and frustrated and depressed.

# 38

---

JOURNAL: Thursday, September 20

IT WAS AFTER MIDNIGHT WHEN THE BUS GOT INTO Shelby. I took a room at the Blue Cloud Hotel. I feel a lot better now, after a couple of days of good rest and no bad dreams.

They call this town the Gateway to Alaska, only I'm not going to Alaska. They also call it the Sports Center of Northern Montana, but that doesn't do me much good either, since I'm not very sports-minded. But I've always liked boxing and found out that on the Fourth of July, 1923, Jack Dempsey fought Tommy Gibbons for the world's heavyweight title right here in Shelby. Jack won the 15-rounder by a decision. An old-timer at the hotel—he must be over 90 if he's a day—told me he was there and saw the fight in this big wooden arena they built to hold 40,000 people for the fight. The old guy says he was right down at ringside when Dempsey got hit, real hard, and some of Dempsey's sweat flopped onto him. Says he didn't wash for a month. I found that to be sickening.

There's a new Robin Williams comedy at the mall here in town and I'm going to see it this afternoon. Might cheer me up. I don't like being Old Mr. Grumpy. Not in my nature. I'm usually full of optimism, an open kind of person, and I just won't allow myself to become a victim of depression.

\* \* \*

The Robin Williams picture was just what I needed. Robin played a nerd who inherits this musty old castle in Transylvania and he tries to turn it into a resort hotel, a kind of Club Med thing. But he doesn't know that the place originally belonged to Count Dracula and that there are still vampires in the cellar. They keep sucking the blood out of Robin's guests which reduces his business, but before Robin can do anything to get rid of them, he falls for a lady vampire. She bites his neck and ole Robin is turned into a vampire himself! Then he loses his fangs in a car accident so he doesn't have any to bite with.

The whole thing was a laugh riot. I left the theater feeling peppy and refreshed. Just the tonic I needed to throw off all those negative thoughts!

There are fine days ahead. I just have to keep the faith. Good things are going to happen in Montana. And good begets good.

That's what my mother always said.

# 39

FOUR DAYS HAD PASSED SINCE PAUL VENTRY HAD met with Sheriff Longbow at the sheriff's station, and although the rancher kept telling himself that Amy was all right, that they'd hear from her soon, his thoughts constantly returned to the dream of the black train. He kept reliving the scene inside the coach, reexperiencing the agony in Amy's face, hearing the terror in her voice. And he kept asking himself, what can I do? What can I do?

He moved through his work like an automaton; it was almost impossible to think about sheep ranching when each day held no word from Amy.

Josh was deeply concerned about his father. The Paul Ventry he had known no longer existed—the man who had gloried in the brute wildness of Montana, who knew every mile of plain and grassland, every river and creek, who had a truly heartfelt love of the wild country, and who nurtured a fierce pride in his role as a sheepman.

Josh recalled campfire nights with his father, when Paul Ventry would talk of the changing color of mountain shadows, of the suppleness of spruce trees as they bent gracefully to the wind, of the incredible cloud shapes in the wide arc of Montana sky, of pink dawns and red-gold sunsets.

Now, none of these things mattered to the veteran rancher.

"Dad, are you all right?" Josh asked him.

"No, I'm not all right," Paul Ventry replied. "And I won't be until I know that your sister is safe."

Josh was frustrated. His sister was probably fine. Independent and strong-willed, she could take care of herself. Amy had bested him several times in wrestling matches that were playful brother-sister rivalries on one hand, but serious competitions on the other. Josh was sure that nothing had happened to her.

But he was wrong.

That same afternoon Dave Hallenbeck appeared at the Ventry ranch. He had ridden over from his own spread at Wolf Fork, and after dismounting, he took a parcel from his saddlebag.

Josh had seen Hallenbeck coming up the driveway and immediately notified his father. They met the visitor on the wide, shaded veranda of the house and invited him inside.

"No, this isn't a social call," said the cattleman. He was a big man, well past middle age, but still capable of spending many hours in the saddle without tiring; it was a long ride from Wolf Fork. "I came to give you this."

He handed the wrapped object to Paul Ventry.

"Found it early this morning up in the mountains," said Hallenbeck. "I thought you'd want to see it."

Paul pulled away the wrapping, drawing in a sharp breath of pain. Amy's cream-colored purse, the one he'd given her as a going-away present. It had been brutally savaged, ripped and twisted. Inside it: lipstick, a comb . . . and a plastic wallet organizer filled with photos and candid snapshots of the Ventry family.

"I knew it was your daughter's from the pictures," said the cattleman softly. "Figured you'd want me to bring it here first, instead of takin' it direct to the sheriff."

Josh stood there as stunned as his father; his voice trembled. "Those dark stains—"

"Blood," said Paul Ventry numbly. "Amy's blood."

"I'm real sorry," Hallenbeck murmured, "I really am."

Paul Ventry swallowed, fixed his eyes on the cattleman. "Where exactly did you find it?"

"Near Harper's Creek at the top of the ridge. Can't figure how it got way up there. It's wild country."

"I thank you kindly for bringing this to me," said Ventry, his voice tight. He was obviously struggling for emotional control.

Josh had taken Amy's purse from his father and was examining it.

"Those toothmarks," Hallenbeck said, "I figure they come from a bear, most likely. Got some mean ones up in the Belt."

A silence, as the three men pondered the situation.

"Still can't figure it," said Hallenbeck, shaking his head. "How it got up there."

"Someone took her into the mountains," said Paul Ventry.

"You mean, Amy was kidnapped?" asked Hallenbeck.

"That's what I mean."

"Well, I sure as God hope she's still okay," said the cattleman. "And that you find her."

"I don't think we'll find her," said Paul softly. "I think it's too late."

"What makes you say that?"

Paul Ventry smiled thinly. "Because she told me so."

## 40

JOURNAL, continued:

I GUESS YOU KNOW BY NOW THAT I'M A SUCKER FOR those true crime books. (Especially the ones about serial killers.) But I usually end up not really enjoying the books because they make me sick reading about these nutcase guys who go around slaughtering people.

Of course, whoever reads this journal might scoff at me and claim I'm no different from those others because I keep on killing people just like the wackos in the books. But the difference is quite extraordinary.

If you are reading these words you will recall that I have covered this argument in earlier pages, but I'm willing to elaborate and extend myself on this theme to head off any unjust criticism. I do not enjoy being thought of as some kind of maniac.

The book I refer to now was about Ted Bundy, the guy they executed in the postscript. (I mean, the final chapter of the book tells about his being executed by legal means.)

Hey, I'm glad he's dead! He had no mental control. (One look at those eyes of his on the book cover will tell you that.) He did things like cutting off the heads of about a dozen or so coeds. They were his specialty. He killed about 36 of them, total. And he did other sicko stuff like biting into the buttocks of one girl. They found his teethmarks there. You just can't let someone like that go on living.

Back to *me*, right? How come I deserve to live and Bundy doesn't, right? Well, the truth is that, as you know by now, I am acting under a compulsive personality disorder which I am certain is self-curable and which, once I get it under full control, will be totally erased from my daily activities, allowing me to contribute to the world as a citizen of this great country of ours. (And, yes, with all of its flaws, this country *is* great, make no mistake, and I'm proud to be a part of it.)

So, you ask, what about the people I have already killed and the ones ahead who will die before I get this negative side of my personality under control? Don't I deserve to be executed just like Ted Bundy because of what I've done? No. Not at all. Several of what you might term my "victims" deserved to die (like that biker and the homosexual) or did things to directly encourage my killing them, thus bringing the real cause of their death upon themselves. It's like the old story of the guy who walks around a corner and an upstairs safe falls on him. When you really analyze the situation logically, you have to conclude that it's all *his* fault. He made the decision to be in that particular spot, at exactly that moment. He didn't *have* to turn that corner, did he? It was his own decision. And the moral is that we must all accept responsibility for our actions, and for the consequences which result.

I feel that Fate has a strong part in what I do regarding this ongoing compulsion of mine. Fate places these particular people—bang!—right in my path. This being the truth, then it can be argued, with solid justification, that I function in these instances as a mere tool of Fate. Therefore, although I am often disturbed by what I perceive as a personality weakness, most of the time I feel no inner sense of personal *guilt*. Truly, I believe these particular people were meant to die at this particular time and I am simply an agent which Fate has chosen to accomplish this action. If they hadn't met me, then a truck would have run over them, or they would have had sudden heart attacks, or their doctors would tell them they had just a few days left to live because of some fatal disease.

Do you see the logic of this? I don't go around cutting

heads off or mutilating people or having some kind of sicko sex with their corpses or biting into their buttocks or any of this kind of really disgusting behavior.

Ted Bundy admitted he liked to read pornography and would seek out these sleaze shops where they sell all this porno stuff and he'd get a kick out of reading about sex tortures and the like. Whew. You know how I feel about porn. It's a blot on our society that needs to be erased—like drug traffic and burning the American flag. Pornography eats away at the moral fiber of this country the same way a bunch of hungry termites eat away at the foundations of a wooden house. Pretty soon, they eat up all the supports and the house falls over.

So Ted Bundy sought out this kind of filth because he was an abnormal. In the end, he was cutting off girls' heads. So there you are.

In this latest book I just read on Bundy he talks to these two reporters about his killing self like it was somebody else entirely he was describing. Which means he could not talk about what he did in an honest, direct fashion the way I am doing in this journal.

I leave it to you. Which one of us is the sicko?

As the lawyers say, I rest my case.

# 41

JOURNAL: Friday, September 21

ANOTHER BAD DREAM. REALLY BAD. IN FACT, I'M writing this entry at 3 a.m. in the morning because the nightmare woke me up and I can't get back to sleep, thinking about it. So I may as well write it down.

It started real ordinary. The scary ones all seem to start that way, easy and natural, and they gradually slip into the awful parts, taking you along into a dark area you don't want to get into, that you are terrified of, and would never go to if you weren't dreaming.

This one began in warm yellow sunlight, with me walking along a road that cut through this piney wood. (There were other kinds of trees there, too, but I don't know much about different trees so I can't say what they were.) Anyway, there were plenty of trees, with a mass of thick pine needles, under my feet, and with heavy green foliage everywhere. There was the crisp smell of sunlight and the church smell of the pines and the cheeping of birds. All straight out of a kid's picture book, and that's what I think inspired this part of the dream, because I remember when I was seven, that Gramps bought me this picture book of forests around the world, and I just got entirely lost in that book, trying to imagine what it would be like to walk through those thick, magical-looking forests, all alone, with nobody knowing I was there, deep inside the woods, with the tall trees all around me.

And that's how it was in this dream—just me alone at age seven, in this pine forest, enjoying the peace and quiet. But then it started getting dark. Fast. A lot faster than in real life. All the birds stopped singing and the sun dropped out of the sky like a falling stone. The path I was on narrowed, and the trees seemed to be pressing in closer. And it got cold. A wind had come swirling up, with voices in it, crying Run, Eddie! Something bad is coming, Eddie! Better run, boy! Catch you if you don't run fast. Run!

And I took off like a stepped-on cat. Started booting it along that path with tree branches whipping at me, slashing at my face and cutting my shirt like swords. I was crying by then, and really scared, because the whole forest seemed to be coming alive and the trees all had mouths full of sharp teeth, like daggers, and now they were leaning over to bite at my flesh. I felt pain and blood was running into my eyes, blinding me.

Then I saw a cabin. Just ahead, with the path going right up to the door. It was open. I ran inside, slamming the door behind me and leaning against it, sobbing and shaking all over.

Suddenly I wasn't a seven-year-old kid anymore. I was me, now, at my age, and I was buck naked. My flesh (no cuts or blood!) was puckered with the cold as the night wind sliced through the cracks in the cabin's roof and walls.

Then I realized (the way you do in dreams) that a big deeply-upholstered chair (we had one back in Kansas) was directly in front of the fireplace and I hunched down in that chair, pressing against the cushions for warmth, shivering, with my arms crossed over my chest. There was no warmth from the fireplace—only dead black ashes.

That's when I heard the sound of something coming out of the forest toward the cabin. Clump, clump, clump. Heavy footsteps. Heading for me.

Coming for me.

Something awful.

And getting closer every second.

I was sweating. As cold as it was, I was in a sweat of fear.

My eyes searched for escape. There was no back door to the place, no windows. What could I do? Where could I go?

Then the door bulged. Like it was under a terrible pressure. Something was bending it inward. A deep voice, old and raspy, cried out. Let me in, Eddie! Open the door!

I jumped from the chair and ran to the far wall, pressing my back against the rough wood, my eyes bugging as the door just *exploded* open.

And Gramps was there. Just like in the carnival dream. Only instead of carrying a chicken he had a long dark green coat over his arm. He was smiling at me.

Nothing to be afraid of, boy. It's just me an' your Mom.

And that's when I saw that it wasn't a coat over his arm. It was my mother's body, loose like a sack and dark green with grave mold. Dark green and rotting.

Your mama's hungry, boy. I brought her here for a feed. She needs to eat.

And he walked over and grabbed me by the neck and kind of draped my mother's body around me, with her rotted arms hanging over my shoulders and her moldy legs pressing against my naked skin. The stink that came off her was the stink of the grave, of deep earth and things long dead.

I was helpless. Then, slowly, her head raised itself and her dead face was right in front of *my* face, maybe an inch away, and she was smiling a broken-toothed idiot's smile and her eyes were filmed with red, wormy veins, and I could see her tongue moving like a fat dark snake inside the rotted cavern of her mouth.

Eddie . . . my little boy. Didn't I always take care of you, sweetie? Now it's your turn to take care of your Mommy . . .

And she buried her teeth in my neck, ripping out a huge gobbet of my flesh and starting to chew . . .

Which is when I woke up here in the motel, covered with cold slimy sweat. My muscles were twitching and I could hardly breathe.

It was one of the worst nightmares I've ever had.

Now, why would I ever have a dream about being devoured by my mother's corpse? She's not even dead, for one thing. Why should I dream of her being dead? There's no reason on earth I should have a dream like this. No reason.

The science people tell us that if we don't dream every night we go crazy. That our minds need to let off steam, as it were, and that dreaming is natural for everybody. Maybe. But I hate having dreams I can't control and being a victim to them. Having dreams is supposed to keep you from going nuts, but what if they *make* you nuts? I mean, if I had dreams as bad as this every night I'd go insane. And I very much want to retain my sanity.

# 42

JOURNAL: Sunday, September 23

I HAD THE DREAM ABOUT MY MOTHER TWO DAYS ago and I think I've figured it out. For one thing, I consider myself on the level of a professional shrink (which is why I'd never go to one). I've always been able to study people and know what makes them tick, and I am quite good at reading beneath the surface of a person.

So I analyzed my dream in relation to my inner self. I think there must be a deep-buried part of me that thinks my mother was kind of smothering me, that she fed off me emotionally after my father began treating her so bad, beating her up and everything. Not that she was the huggy-kissy type. Not at all. She didn't like any open affection, no outward displays. But, inside, I think she turned to me as a kind of replacement for my father. It was subtle, but it was there, and I sensed it somehow, even as a kid.

For example, she didn't like sharing me with anybody. When Gramps would come over (even Mom called him that) and he'd want to take me home with him for the weekend, take me to the park for ice cream and a ride on the big merry-go-round they had there, she always said no, I couldn't go with him to his house because I had to do chores over the weekend. Once every summer she did let me go out to a cabin Gramps had rented near a lake in the woods (the cabin in my dream looked a lot like it) and I had some great times swimming out there and eating the fresh peach ice cream that Gramps made himself.

I have one bad memory connected with the lake. It was what I did to a litter of pups, six of them. I put them all in a cardboard box and then took them to the edge of the long wooden dock and pushed the pups under the water, one by one. When bubbles didn't come up anymore I knew they were dead. I can't remember exactly why I did that except for the power feeling it gave me, that charge I get as I'm taking a life, that's still with me, even today. It's not a sexual thing, not like the wet dreams I used to have as a kid, and it doesn't give me a hard-on. It's more like what I've heard from people who take drugs—a sudden high, a rush of pure pleasure. You kind of tingle all over.

Killing has always given me that. Which is one reason it's so hard to quit.

But getting back to the dream . . . I suppose it came from my subconscious, based on that deep-down feeling that Mom used me as a kind of emotional *food* when I was a kid. The dream makes some sense on that basis.

I feel better now, having figured it out. It was still terrible, having it, and I hope I don't have any more like it, but at least I've got it analyzed.

And I'm proud of myself for that.

# 43

JOURNAL, continued:

WELL, THINGS ARE HEATING UP HERE IN MONTANA, and I'm not talking about the weather. It was dumb of me to kill Norma Jeans, knowing that her dad ran the local newspaper in Malta. That was just plain dumb. I could have picked somebody who wasn't connected with the press. Her old man, Gideon Jeans, naturally is tight with the local police, and when his daughter didn't come home they got out major search parties, led by old Gideon himself. Didn't take long for them to find her in that canyon. (That was *double* dumb. I should have buried her.)

So they found the body, and old man Jeans had a field day with it in his paper, calling for statewide action, and linking his daughter's murder to the stranglings of the two women in Butte and Bozeman. Those Malta headlines about "The Big Sky Strangler" got all the other papers fired up and here I was, sitting in a coffee shop in Conrad (where I'd hitched down Interstate 15 from Shelby), looking at one of those composite police drawings they make up from what witnesses describe. (This was made up from what the waiter in the steak house said in Malta, the one who waited on us at dinner, and from an old lady who'd seen me carry that woman's packages in Butte and get into her Toyota, and from a married couple who'd seen me come out of that apartment complex in Bozeman after strangling the one that worked at the Handi-Serve.)

Anyhow, I stared hard at this composite drawing and had to admit it *did* look a lot like me, with my kind of pointy chin and flat nose and longish thick hair and all. Even the eyes looked like my eyes. Not exactly, but still close. (I could never figure out how these police artists are able to draw a picture of somebody they've never seen. I know they flash different sets of eyes and chins and ears on a screen and ask their witness if these are the ears and so on, but you'd think they wouldn't come so close, the way they do, to the actual killer. It's weird, almost spooky the way they do it.)

And the witnesses even described the kind of clothes I wore, which means I have to buy some new stuff. Boy, the whole thing is just depressing.

# 44

THE SEARCH FOR AMY VENTRY WAS PERSONALLY conducted by John Longbow. It was thorough and painstaking. Several hundred citizens were enlisted to back up the local authorities and they combed the entire area near Harper's Creek as well as a wide stretch of the surrounding Little Belt range.

They found nothing.

After four days and nights, Longbow called off the search, phoning the Ventry ranch from his office in Lewistown.

"We've done all we can at this point," the sheriff told Paul Ventry. "If she *had* been kidnapped for money, I think you'd've heard from her captors by now."

"You're right," said the rancher. "I think she's dead. Someone on that steamer killed her."

"You know I can't accept that theory, Paul."

"Then what do *you* think happened to my daughter?" Ventry's tone was cold.

"She could have been waylaid on the platform at Bitterroot," said the sheriff. "Maybe by a road bum, a roving tramp who saw her alone at the depot after midnight and wanted the money in her purse."

"Then how did it end up in the mountains near Harper's Creek?"

"After he . . . finished with her . . . then he probably

carried her purse up there with him, took out the money and tossed the rest away.''

"If that's true, why didn't you find the rest of the contents in the area? There was a set of makeup containers that Josh gave her for Christmas—and a perfume bottle that Sarrie gave her. And her Girl Scout knife. She never went anywhere without it.''

"Look, Paul,'' sighed the sheriff. "I don't have any answers for you. Could be a bear found the purse after it had been discarded close to the depot, then carried it into the mountains. Maybe some of her stuff fell out on the way.''

"That doesn't sound logical,'' said Ventry.

"You asked me what I think and I'm telling you. Truth is, nobody *knows* what happened.''

"It has to do with the black steam train,'' said Paul Ventry.

"Look, it's getting late,'' said the sheriff. "I've put in a long, tough day, and I'm bushed. I'm going home and get some shut-eye. I think you could use some yourself.''

"The train is out there, somewhere, and it's the answer to everything.''

"I wish I could believe that.'' The lawman paused. "Good night, Paul. Get some sleep, if you can.''

John Longbow put down the phone, leaned back in his desk chair, and stared at the map of central Montana.

He felt empty and frustrated.

# 45

I WENT TO A SALVATION ARMY STORE HERE IN CONrad and got some pants and shirts and burned the old stuff. So at least the clothes thing is taken care of. I can't do anything about my nose or chin, but I did cut my hair a lot shorter, had a barber do it. He was an old coot, had been in Conrad since, as he put it, "this here town was no more'n a grease spot on the road." He was totally bald himself (meaning at least he didn't have to cut his own hair!) and he was gabbing about the news stories and what did I think about them.

They're just trying to sell papers, I said.

You see the picture of the killer guy?

It wasn't a picture, it was just some drawing the cops made up, I said. They like to get all excited over serial killers.

I dunno, they say at least three different people saw this guy.

Hey, I could find three people right here in town who'll tell you they saw Elvis Presley after he died. People like to talk, get their names in the paper.

I dunno, he repeated.

Montana just wants its own serial killer, I said lightly. So the cops made one up.

I dunno, he said for the third time.

The old geeze was a real pain in the ass.

After the haircut I got what I thought was a terrific idea. I'd go to one of those gag shops where they sell plastic snakes and fake spiders. I'd buy myself a mustache and that would help disguise me.

I found a store in Conrad's only shopping center which sold junk meant mostly for the tourist trade. (They're trying real hard to expand the town.) The window was full of stuff like ashtrays that talk back to you and glasses with holes in the bottom and flowers that squirt water in your face when you lean over to smell them. There were several monster masks in the window also—of the Wolfman and Dracula and that guy Freddy with the razor blades in his glove, and a nice green one, with metal bolts at each side, of Frankenstein. They even had a long-nosed one of Nixon, but I thought that was in bad taste. I don't believe that people should be making fun of our presidents whether they approve of what they did in office or not. Nixon made some mistakes, but hey, who's perfect? And he was terrific in his foreign policy, opening up China and all. We ought to be grateful to him for that.

The middle-aged lady who came to wait on me was using far too much makeup. She looked like a monster herself, with all these colors on her eyes and cheeks and lips. I find it amazing that a woman like that can't just take one look in a mirror and realize how overdone her makeup is. I mean, it's so obvious. Like the wife of that Reverend Bakker guy who's in jail with all the mascara.

When I told her I wanted to see some mustaches she took out a tray full of them and put it on top of the glass counter.

Take your pick, she said, in a bored tone of voice.

I tried one on. It didn't look good. Tried another. No good. They looked phony. Wouldn't fool anybody.

Are these the best you've got? I asked.

What's wrong with them?

They all look phony.

Well, mister, they're the only ones we got. Maybe you'd like to see some beards.

No. No beards, I said. I'll just pass on the whole thing.

She glared at me as I walked out of the store. I almost turned around to say, you wear too much makeup, lady. But I didn't. No use hurting her feelings. You can't change a woman like that. They get angry or they get hurt, but they don't improve.

In the shopping center, as I was walking toward the stairs leading down, a man stepped directly in front of me. A bald little guy, short like a dwarf, with glittery eyes. He pointed a stubby finger at me.

The Big Sky Strangler, he said.

What? What are you saying? I gaped at him. How did he know me? This was incredible. Several other shoppers turned to watch.

I felt trapped.

He's right here, among us, said the stubby little man, still pointing at me.

I started to push him aside. Maybe I could make a run for the stairs and get to the parking lot and steal a car. It was a crazy plan, but this guy had caught me completely off guard.

He's gonna kill again! the little man declared, gripping my arm. His eyes rolled in his head.

Get out of my way, I snapped, ready to make my run.

I know him! raved the little man. He's an alien from out of space. From a far galaxy. Came down in a flying saucer. He's bulletproof. And he can fly!

The shoppers began turning away, embarrassed. I relaxed, sighing in relief. Shorty was a walking nutcase. Every city has them. They go around muttering and shouting insane stuff all day and people try to ignore them.

Maybe you should call the space patrol, I told the man. They have ways of catching aliens. They use space nets.

Good idea! he said. That's a *very* good idea, sir. I shall let the space patrol deal with him. May I thank you, citizen, for this excellent suggestion.

My pleasure, I said. And went down the stairs.

I decided to forget about wearing a fake mustache.

# 46

---

DESPITE PROTESTS FROM THE STEADILY INCREASING membership of Citizens for a Clean Environment, Mitchell Mining continued to expand its local operations. Blair Mitchell stood resolute against all opposition, whether public or—via his daughter—private.

Cris Mitchell, while unsurprised at her father's determination, was nevertheless frustrated. She'd even considered the possibility of giving a candid (and unfavorable) interview to the local paper—an idea she rejected only because of her deep love for her father. Finally, in desperation, she phoned Josh.

"I know you're going through hell right now, and I don't want to add to the pressure, but I don't know any other way. I need to talk, Josh. It's important."

They sat in her van, talking in the moonlight just off Main Street.

"I've been going to some CFCE meetings," she said. "We're getting more members all the time, and support is really building in the community. But there's no strong leadership. Without you there, everything is disorganized. We need you to take charge. Otherwise, there's a good chance Dad will win."

"I can't," he said, shaking his head. "Since Amy left, my workload at the ranch has doubled. Now with her missing . . ." His voice broke. ". . . with her maybe dead, I've got to take care of my own dad, too. He's gone around the bend, Cris. He's completely lost in this steam train thing of his. He doesn't *act* crazy, but he *talks* crazy, and I don't know what to do.'' In despair, Josh lowered his head into his hands. Cris reached over and began gently stroking his back.

"I shouldn't have asked you,'' she said. ''It was insensitive of me. I'm sorry."

He looked up at her. "I'm still as dedicated to saving the Little Belt as I ever was. But until we *know* what happened to Amy, everything else just has to be put on hold. The CFCE will have to function without me.''

Cris looked at him tenderly. ''Just as long as you don't ask *me* to function without you."

And she leaned over to kiss his lips.

# 47

RAILROAD AUTHORITIES VERIFIED THE SHERIFF'S AS-
sertion that no commercial steam trains were running in the
state. "Only place in the world that runs regular steamers
these days is China," Sheriff Longbow reported to Paul Ventry. "In this country, we got a few, but they're all for tourists.
There's one in South Dakota and another on a Colorado–New
Mexico run down in the Four Corners area. None in Montana."

"Then what about a privately owned steamer, part of somebody's collection?" Ventry asked.

"One way or another, somebody official would know about
it," Longbow replied. "Has to be that Amy was mistaken."

But Paul Ventry persisted in his belief that the black
steamer was real. He was now spending his daylight hours
inside the Lewistown public library, a large fieldstone building on the corner of Main and Seventh Avenue South, con-
ducting a blind search in the hope that he'd uncover
information that would help support his case with Longbow.
Each day he sat at the long wooden reading table in the library's Reference Room, poring over back issues of the *News-
Argus*.

His initial research into the rail history of the area expanded
to news accounts dealing with reports of missing persons in
north central Montana, the six-county area surrounding Lewistown.

By the end of the second day he felt he'd struck pay dirt. A pattern was emerging. In seven cases over the past five years involving individuals reported missing in the area, four of these people were known to have been traveling by train. An extraordinarily high percentage given the fact that travel by rail was a rare form of transportation in modern-day Montana.

Ventry carefully copied names, dates, locations, case details. When he was satisfied that he had enough data, he would take his findings to John Longbow.

# 48

_____

JOURNAL, continued:

THERE'S A FEELING IN MONTANA THAT YOU'RE
back in the Old West. Lot of the men wear cowboy hats and
walk around in fancy cowhide boots. Every town you go to
is full of Western artifacts and every area has its Western
ghost town. It's kind of like the Civil War is in the South.
You go there and it seems the war just ended about a month
ago. People still talk about it and there's souvenirs and Con-
federate flags and banners everywhere. In Montana, it's real
John Wayne country, the Old West come alive. Including a
lot of rodeos.

There was one going on here in Conrad, just a mile or two
beyond the main part of town, and I decided it might be fun
to go see it. Get my mind off what the papers were saying.
I'd never been to a rodeo. Had read about them and seen
movies. In fact, I remember one with Steve McQueen in it.
He played a guy named Junior somebody and I enjoyed
watching that one.

I found out that a rodeo is a lot like going to a circus.
Everything is noisy, with bucking horses and cowgirls in
flashy spangled outfits and bright-painted clowns for the bulls
to chase and big grandstands full of people eating popcorn
and drinking Cokes. (Is there anywhere on this whole planet
where people don't drink Coca-Cola? I've seen photos of

Coke signs in the deserts of Arabia and the jungles of Africa—and you can be sure that when they build a city on Mars the first thing they'll be shipping in is truckloads of Coca-Cola. Me, I'd like to have just a tiny percentage of the profits from these zillions of Cokes they sell all over the world every day. I'd be a rich man.)

I got a pretty good aisle seat in the main grandstand and nibbled on some roasted peanuts and watched whooping cowboys get tossed off fierce-looking bulls. They'd roll their eyes, these big bulls would, with white froth looping from their mouths, and just shake off the riders like water off a dog's back. The second a cowboy hit the dirt a clown would jump out to lure the bull away from the fallen rider—and when the bull went after the clown he'd jump into a barrel and the bull's horns would bang into the wood while the cowboy got up and limped back to the chutes. Not all of them limped, but most did. I couldn't figure why anybody would want to try riding a bull or a wild, crazy-eyed bucking horse. Even when you won, the prizes weren't anything to write home about. There are plenty of broken bones and skull fractures in a rodeo. Dumb way to make a living.

I read somewhere that they use a real tight strap around the balls of the bull to make him jump harder and higher. And they do other things just as bad. This article I read told all about it. I like getting the inside scoop, because there's always more to everything than you see on the surface. (There's sure a lot more to Yours Truly than most people ever see!)

The calf-roping was fun to watch—and these boys could ride and rope like the rest of us breathe air. It was something to see the way they competed against the clock, making every move count. Makes you realize how much time we waste in our lives. What I need in my life right now is a goal to work toward. Not just getting control of the compulsion, I mean having a solid future in mind. But when I try to think of the future it's all blank, like a sheet of white paper. Like getting a fortune cookie in a Chinese restaurant and breaking it open to read your fortune and finding out there's no little slip of paper inside. Just an empty cookie. That's how my whole life seems these days. Like that cookie.

I was thinking such thoughts when I felt a hand touch my left shoulder.

Hi, pardner, you look a mite thirsty. How 'bout a beer?

I looked up at this attractive cowgirl in a short, fringed skirt, white boots decorated with silver stars, a spangled blouse, red bandanna, topped by a wide-brim Western sombrero. A beer tray was balanced from a strap on her shoulder.

I don't like beer, I told her.

That's okay. I've sold enough today. Mind if I sit? I'm kind of tuckered.

I don't mind, I said.

And I moved over on the wooden slat to give her some room. She sat down, slipping the tray from her shoulder and letting it rest against her booted leg. The skin between her shirt and her white boot tops was very tan. A real outdoor Montana type.

You got a cigarette?

I've given up smoking, I told her. Cigarettes can kill you.

Lotta things can kill you, she said. I also drink Scotch whiskey and that can kill me. When I visit my sister in California I could get killed by an earthquake. Or a dog with rabies could bite me. Hell, I could even meet up with the Big Sky Strangler—but right now, I just want a cigarette.

Her remark about meeting the Big Sky Strangler seemed almost surreal. The last thing this woman figured was that she was talking to him right this minute. Strange. Life can be strange.

It wasn't easy for me to quit cigarettes, I told her. It's something I really had to work at.

What do you want from me? she asked sharply, a Boy Scout merit badge?

You can make fun of it if you want to, I said, but I'm proud of what I've done.

She patted my shoulder. You're right, I was just being a bitch. Didn't mean to put you down, darlin', but I get a little testy about this time of day. I tellya, it's no sweet job, lugging this stuff up and down these lousy grandstands, and getting my fanny pinched by drunken cowboys who think I can't wait to climb into the saddle with 'em. Lotta creeps in this world.

I can see how it's a rough job, I told her.

She took off her big white Stetson and pushed at her hair. It was the same color hair as the one that I killed had in Butte, a kind of sandy brown.

I'm gonna take off early, call it a day, she said. Do you like fish?

I blinked. Oh, I guess they're all right. I neither like nor dislike them, I said. I never had one as a pet.

She let out a hoot and slapped her hat against one knee.

No, no, darlin'. What I meant is, do you like *eating* them?

I had to laugh at myself on that one. I'd taken her question in a literal sense. Her personality was throwing me off. I'm never much good with direct women.

My boyfriend, bastard that he is, just rode off into the sunset, leaving me with a fridge full of trout and no one to feed 'em to. So what do you say to a free fish dinner?

I say great, I told her. In fact, I appreciate the offer.

Good. You may be straight arrow, but I think you're cute. She shook my hand and her grip was firm.

I'm Lorry Haines, she said.

Ed Timmons, I said back to her.

I didn't want to eat alone tonight, she said. Now I won't have to.


Lorry Haines drove me to a small yellow frame house trimmed in brown with a neat little fenced yard.

I met Bobby at a rodeo in Billings, she told me as she started dinner. He was a bronc rider, top of his class. Tall and hunky with muscle in all the right places. We hit it off and he asked me to leave town and tour the circuit with him.

Is Billings your home town? I asked.

Yeah. I grew up there. When I met Bobby, I was working in a clothing store. Went to the rodeo that weekend with a girl friend and there was ole Bobby, tall in the saddle, with a glint in his eye. Before the weekend was over I'd agreed to quit my job and follow him around the circuit.

That's when you started selling beer, eh?

Yeah. They always need sales people in the stands. It was easy to get work.

What happened between you and Bobby?

Oh, it was great for awhile. He was Bobby Superstud, knew

just about everything there is to know about giving a girl a good time in the sack.

Uh huh, I said, beginning to feel a little uncomfortable.

But we fought like a couple of bobcats. Over all kinds of stuff. Then, last night, I came home here to this house and found a note from the bastard. A kiss-off note. He just up and took off. Probably with some bimbo he met in town.

Then this place isn't yours?

Nope. I never owned me a house. This belongs to a friend of Bobby's, a retired rodeo rider. He's out of town this weekend, so we got it to use. I'll be leaving tomorrow.

Where will you go?

Who knows? I'm just a rolling stone these days.

Funny, I told her. That's what a lot of people have called me.

Yeah? And she smiled. Just a couple of rolling stones, you and me.

She'd been fixing dinner as we talked, bustling around the kitchen while I sat at a small Formica table in the dining nook. She asked me to help with the salad, so I started cutting up the lettuce she'd washed.

You could always go back to Billings, I said. Aren't your folks still there?

Sure, but we never got along. We're not on what you might call the best of terms. Mom's a real bitch, if you want to know the truth. And Dad's no bargain, either.

So what *are* you going to do?

She turned from the trout, which were browning in the pan, and grinned at me. I dunno, she said. Maybe I'll join a convent.

I grinned back at that. Yeah. I can see you as the praying cowgirl nun!

I know one damn thing, she said. After tomorrow, I'm finished with rodeos.

The food was ready and she laid it out on the table. We sat down and began eating. The trout was great—covered in cornmeal, all brown and crusty, just the way I like it—and I told her so.

Thanks, pardner! she said.

We ate in silence for awhile, then she canted her head and gave me a little cat-grin.

Anybody ever tell you how cute you are?

I knew it was coming, but it still shook me. This direct sexual approach. Like that older woman in Butte. I didn't know how to handle it. I never have.

*You're* the cute one, I said. Bet a lot of guys have been after you since you grew up.

She bit into a dinner roll. Then she took a swallow of coffee. Then she looked at me again.

You like oral sex? she asked.

*After midnight. Open country under a clouded moon.*
*A boy. Standing on a depot platform.*
*Alone.*
*He turns, startled to see it emerging from the darkness.*
*Breathing in the night, it waits.*
*Motionless.*
*Waiting.*
*The boy approaches, is gathered in, taken, trapped.*
*He struggles, fights for his life. Screams.*
*Blood.*
*The sweet taste of flesh.*

# 49

---

I WOKE UP THIS MORNING ALONE IN BED. LORRY was already dressed and packed.

You better get your butt in gear, darlin', because ole Jeeter, who owns this place, is due back today. And that man can be mean as a snake in a sock. We'd best be gone.

She was right. It would be hard to explain just who I was if this Jeeter guy showed, so I took a fast shower, got dressed, gobbled down the breakfast Lorry had fixed for me (great little cook!) and we got out of there.

We'd talked in bed after we had sex. About the future. About us pairing up on the road. Just two rolling stones. It sounded good to me at the time, since the sex with Lorry had been real fine and I needed somebody like her to help me straighten out. Naturally I didn't tell her about the compulsion, or that I'd ever killed anybody.

The thing is, and I know whoever reads this will get a big laugh out of it, but the thing is I was in love. For the first time in my whole life. Truly in love. They say that love can strike like lightning, that one minute you're not in love and the next minute you are. And that's how it happened with me and Lorry. There was something about her that ignited my blood. I don't mean just the great sex we had, I mean her whole *being*. She gave off a kind of wondrous aura. I don't

163

expect you to understand because I don't myself. But it happened, and a fact is a fact.

Lorry owned an orange VW—a Volkswagen bug. I'd never driven one before and I was not impressed with its performance. It had so little power that it was almost impossible to pass other cars on the Interstate.

A bug's not supposed to be fast, she told me with a grin. This is no sports car. VWs were made to *last*. This one's twenty-five years old.

She told me she'd owned it for the last three years and it had never given her any mechanical trouble.

I don't like it, I said. Ted Bundy drove a Volkswagen.

Who?

The guy that killed all those coeds, I told her. Cut their heads off, on a lot of them. He drove a gold VW.

So he drove a bug, she said. So what? It's not going to turn you into a mass murderer.

I blinked at that. Talking to her about Bundy was stupid. I had to avoid that kind of talk.

I want you to sell it, I said.

*Sell* it! Her voice jumped up a couple of octaves. You gotta be nuts. I'm not selling my bug.

I didn't look at her, just kept driving. I'd made her angry. Our first day together and already we were fighting.

When we get into Great Falls, I said, I want you to find a dealer and get rid of this car.

You're *serious*, aren't you?

Yes.

But Eddie, we need wheels. If we're gonna travel around together we need a car.

Fine. Buy another. Just so it isn't a VW.

A silence. Then she said, hard-toned: And what if I say no?

Then we split.

Over a *car*! Her brows were lifted in astonishment.

I took the next off ramp from I-15 and pulled to a stop on an access road under a big tree. Then I turned off the engine and reached for her. She came into my arms smooth as butter. I kissed away the frown between her eyes. She kissed me back. Things were a lot better.

I'm really not trying to give you a bad time, I said. It's just that whenever I'm in this car I'll be thinking of Ted Bundy and what he did to those coeds—and I don't want to do that.

She nestled her head against my shoulder.

Okay, she said, if it bothers you so much, I'll sell the bug.

Then she raised her head and looked at me. You know, Eddie, you're a strange guy.

I nodded. I never said I wasn't.

I'm not going to let what we've got go to hell over a car, she said. Already, you're very special to me.

When I came to Montana, I said to her, I never thought I'd get into a heavy relationship. It's kinda spooky.

I think I love you, she said.

I think I love you, too, I told her.

She nestled deeper into my shoulder. It was a fine fall day, cool and crisp. A slight breeze ruffled her hair against my cheek. I had my arm around her and I guess we looked like something out of one of those Norman Rockwell paintings.

I want to know all about you, Lorry said. I don't know anything. What was your childhood like?

I don't want to get into that kind of stuff, I said. Not now.

She didn't argue, just closed her eyes and let the breeze blow over us under that big Montana sky.

I sat there in the silent VW with her head pressing against my shoulder wondering if this was the karma that Kathleen Kelly told me I'd find here in Montana. Was this the answer to my problem? Was this what I came here for? And what about the future? Could I have a real future—a loving future—with Lorry Haines? A man like me?

*Could* I?

I started the engine of the VW, then headed back for the Interstate. We would have to live the future hour by hour, day by day.

And the compulsion. What about the killings? Maybe, with Lorry in my life, I could find a way to stop.

Maybe.

## 50

THAT NIGHT AT THE RANCH PAUL VENTRY SHOWED his son what he'd discovered.

"I still don't have everything I need to convince Longbow," said the veteran rancher, "but it's coming together."

Josh looked up from the stack of Xeroxed news clippings. He frowned, easing back in his chair. "There's nothing here, Dad."

"Nothing!" Paul Ventry's face reddened with anger. "All those missing people, all here in north central Montana, and all of 'em connected with trains!"

"You still don't know *why* they're listed as missing," said Josh.

"The steamer," nodded his father. "They got on board and never got off."

"There's no mention in any of these articles of a steam train," declared Josh. "You're just trying to—"

"Then you don't see the *pattern*?" demanded Ventry.

"Dad . . . there's no pattern."

"The hell there isn't!" snapped the veteran as he scooped up the clippings. "You just refuse to see it."

"I'd like to be able to believe you," said Josh softly. "But I can't." He looked steadily at his father. "Dad, how long do you intend to keep chasing something that doesn't exist?"

"Long enough to prove that it *does*," Paul Ventry said, leaving Josh to stare sadly after him as he walked stiffly from the room.

# 51

JOURNAL, continued:

AS A NATIVE MONTANAN, LORRY KNEW GREAT
Falls. She was my own personal tour guide, telling me things
as we drove.

Got its name, she said, from the Lewis and Clark Expe-
dition when ole Meriwether Lewis walked out of camp one
summer morning in 1805, following the sound of a tremen-
dous roar along the river. That's when he discovered what he
called The Great Falls of the Missouri. Big dam is there now.

Is it still worth looking at? I asked Lorry.

You bet, she said. It's a guaranteed sight.

You know, I told her, I've always had a yen to go white
water rafting down the Colorado River, along the Grand Canyon and all.

Sounds like fun. We can do it together, she said.

The scenery around us was postcard perfect. Off to the
west the Rockies took a big hike into the sky and to the east
were vast wheat fields and rolling prairies.

How big is Great Falls? I asked.

Pretty big for Montana, she said. More than seventy thousand, last time I heard. People just like the location, the way
it's set between Glacier and Yellowstone. And the winters are
not all that bad here, because of the chinooks.

The what?

Warm winds that blow down off the slopes of the Rockies. You never heard of 'em?

Never, I said.

Now we were into town, with Lorry pointing out various sights as we drove past.

That's the Russell Museum, she said. You know, the famous Western artist, Charles M. Russell. He lived here in Great Falls. His paintings are worth a fortune.

I think I've seen some of his stuff, I said.

This would be a nice place to raise kids, Lorry said.

I never wanted kids, I told her, my voice taking on a sharp note. If you're looking to have kids by me, you've got the wrong stud.

Hey, don't take everything so personal, she said. I was just talking about what kind of a place this is. It's a *family* kind of town.

What about you, I asked. Did you ever want children?

I guess every woman wants children at some time or other—but I don't think I'd make a very good mother, she said.

Maybe not, I said.

We found a motel with a long wooden rail in front and three big plaster horses hitched to it. The place was called (you guessed it) The Hitching Post. Another touch of the Old West.

We booked a room there and spent most of the afternoon having sex.

She was great in bed. I'd never felt so free before when I'd been with a woman. With Lorry, everything was different. Easier. More comfortable. And a whole lot more fun.

We had a TV in our room and Lorry was watching the news when I came out of the bathroom, rubbing my head with a towel. They had a picture of the Big Sky Strangler on the screen. I threw the towel aside and sat down on the bed, staring at the composite drawing, asking myself, does it really look like me? How *much* does it look like me?

I don't know how they expect to catch him from that sketch, Lorry said. He could be any one of ten thousand guys. What they need is a long scar on his cheek, or a harelip, or something.

I was calm. Inside me, there was no feeling of connection with the news story.

The anchorwoman was talking about how police throughout the state of Montana were looking for the killer.

How do they know he's still around here? I said. He could be halfway across the country by now.

Lorry didn't reply. She was listening as the woman reported that authorities figured that the same killer was responsible for yet another murder. The police had discovered the strangled body of a 12-year-old girl in Dodson, not far from Malta. She'd been dumped in a trash bin behind a drugstore.

When they showed the little girl's photo I jumped from the bed, walked over and snapped off the television set. I was furious and my heart was pumping fast.

Lorry complained. Hey! I was watching that. What's wrong with you? Why did you turn it off?

My hands were fisted. I was half-shouting at her. Because they're lying! That . . . guy they're after . . . he'd *never* kill a 12-year-old!

Lorry stared at me. How do *you* know?

I hesitated. I realized that my sudden anger had put me in a tricky spot with her. I took in a couple of deep breaths to steady myself.

Well . . . because . . . his other victims were all much older. Why would he start killing children? It doesn't fit his pattern.

Lorry shook her head. Who knows what a crazy person is going to do next? she said. I can't understand why you're so upset.

I . . . I just get emotionally involved with this kind of thing. I don't like the way they exploit these deaths.

Murder is news, she said. When a serial killer is on the loose, people deserve to know. They *need* to, for their own self-protection.

What do they all plan to do—carry guns around? I asked.

People deserve to know, Lorry insisted. Now can we watch the rest of the news?

Sure, I said, slumping into a chair. I felt exhausted, drained of energy.

I'd have to be more careful around Lorry in the future.

# 52

JOURNAL: Wednesday, September 26

WE SOLD THE VW. LORRY HAD A PRETTY FAIR IDEA of what the car was worth, even as old as it was, and she didn't like what the first two used car lots offered her for it.

These VWs can run forever, she told me. This one's in real sharp condition. Had a complete engine overhaul last year. Got another hundred thousand miles in it at least.

Then we saw this lot with big colored banners and a blinking neon sign:

FRED FARLEY IS FAIR!
TOP DOLLAR FOR YOUR CAR!
YOU CAN TRUST FAIR FREDDY!

Pull in here, Lorry told me.

I did, and by the time I'd cut the engine a tall skinny guy in a dark business suit topped by a white ten-gallon hat comes out of this wooden shack to look at the VW. He's all smiles.

Howdy there, good people! I'm Fred Farley. The folks around here call me Fair Freddy.

He didn't impress me much. Just another cheap huckster.

I wandered around the lot looking at the cars he had for sale while Lorry talked to him about the VW. Some of the cars looked okay, but there were plenty of junkers.

When I got back to Lorry she was shaking hands with Farley. They both seemed satisfied.

We've made a deal, she told me. Mr. Farley says he'll swap even—my VW for the red Mazda pickup. What do you think?

Okay with me, I said.

As she was filling out the paperwork inside the shack I sized up the Mazda. I didn't like the bench-type front seat. Her legs were shorter than mine, which meant that when she drove, my knees would be in my face. And there was a big dent in the front right fender, and quite a bit of rust along the bottom of the driver's door. But I didn't complain. Anything was better than driving Ted Bundy's VW. That's how I thought of it, as *his*. If she'd traded it for a hay wagon I would have kept my mouth shut.

We were moving along the Missouri River and Lorry was driving the pickup. It had more snap than the bug but it was still sluggish. And the front seat *was* uncomfortable.

You look kinda sour, Lorry said. I hope you're not gonna tell me the Boston Strangler drove a Mazda.

I grinned. Lorry could be pretty funny and I have always admired a good sense of humor.

It's not the pickup, I told her. There's nothing wrong with it.

Then what's bugging you?

I'm hungry, I said.

I was, but that wasn't what was bothering me. I'd been fighting back the compulsion all morning. It was spreading inside me, growing like a kind of dark fungus, getting more intense with each passing hour. I guess that's the way a heroin addict feels when the need for a fix begins to take over his body. The feeling just kind of overwhelms everything else.

What worried me—and still worries me as I write these words—is that instead of lessening after each kill, the compulsion was coming back stronger than before. As if each time I killed someone I was feeding it, making it grow.

For the first time since I came to Montana I wondered if I *could* control this disorder of mine.

Which is really frightening to consider.

* * *

We found a cheap, family-type steak house and Lorry ordered a T-bone while I ordered a tuna salad.

Is that all you're going to eat? she asked me. I thought you were hungry.

I am, I told her, but I decided just this week to quit eating dead animals. That's what steak is, you know. A dead cow.

That's crazy! she snapped. Tuna is *fish*. They're animals, too. And they're right there in your salad, dead as any cow.

It's not the same, I said. They fill cows with all kinds of chemicals in their food. You can get cancer and heart trouble and all kinds of other diseases from eating meat. And the animal fat is almost pure cholesterol. It's a scientific fact that vegetarians have the best health of anybody. I've been giving the whole thing a lot of thought lately and I've decided not to eat any more steaks or hamburgers or bacon or ham. It's a decision I made.

You're a weird dude, Eddie, she said.

There's nothing weird about not eating meat, I said. A lot of people are becoming vegetarians now. It's in the magazines and newspapers and on the news and everything. I just want to be healthy and live to be a hundred.

Don't we all? she said. Well, she added, not actually a hundred. That's too old. Nobody wants to be a walking corpse.

She ordered strawberry ice cream for dessert. As she was eating it she looked up at me. You don't trust me, do you? she said.

Why do you say that?

If you trusted me, you'd tell me what's been bugging you. Ever since we got to Great Falls, something has been bugging you. I got rid of the VW, so it can't be that.

I'm just a little tired, I said. Then I grinned at her, trying for some lightness. I've been in bed a lot, I said, but I haven't been sleeping much.

She grinned back.

And rubbed her hand over my crotch.

*Hunting.*
*Roaming the night.*
*Searching for prey.*

# 53

---

JOURNAL, continued:

WE WERE PARKED AT A SPOT OVERLOOKING THE Missouri River. No other cars around. The sky above us was like an immense sheet of black glass punched through with stars. Below us, we could hear the sound of water going past.

Lorry had her head against my shoulder and I could smell the fresh-washed scent of her hair. I would have been enjoying it, except for what was building up inside me.

The compulsion.

You picked the wrong guy to travel with, I finally said. My voice was soft and sad.

Lorry raised her head to look at me. Her eyes burned like jewels in the darkness. I picked the *right* guy, she said.

If you knew me—really knew me—you wouldn't say that, I told her honestly.

So what should I know about you?

The darkness roiling up inside me was blacker than the sky. A whole universe of pressure was engulfing me. Commanding me. I couldn't fight it anymore.

I'm him, I said softly.

Him? She shifted in the seat, sitting up straight. What are you talking about?

The one they're looking for. The one on TV and in the papers. I'm him.

There was a long, strained moment of silence. Lorry's eyes got real intense and I could feel her muscles tighten underneath her clothes. She edged back from me.

Why are you doing this, Eddie? Why are you trying to scare me? I don't like it and it's not funny.

I'm not trying to be funny, I said in the darkness.

Her eyes were wide now. She blinked rapidly. This is . . . for *real*?

For real, I said.

You're—

—the Big Sky Strangler. I finished the sentence for her.

Lorry threw open the Mazda door and jumped out. She began to run along the grass toward the main highway, about a half-mile from where we were parked.

She wasn't hard to catch. Most women aren't. They just don't run the way a man does. Besides, I'm fast. I can move like a lizard when I've a mind to. I caught her before she'd gone five hundred yards.

I grabbed her by the throat, my thumbs in place, ready to dig in. She was shaking and sobbing. Killing her would be easy.

But Lorry was a surprising woman. Suddenly she brought up her right knee in a hard, swift arc and got me right in the balls. I doubled over, gasping, as waves of pain rippled through me.

You sick bastard! she screamed. Goddamn you! She ran back towards the Mazda.

By the time I got there, still dizzy with pain, she'd managed to start the engine and was about to drive off. I grabbed through the open window, fumbling for the ignition key, as she tried to slap my hand away.

Then she lashed out with a fist, catching me a good one across the face. I felt blood running from my mouth. It tasted salty.

Bastard! Bastard! Bastard! She kept screaming the word at me as I pulled the door open and dragged her out. I got her arms pinned, but she was kicking wildly.

I really like you, I told her, spinning her around and punching her in the stomach. Her breath puffed out in a grunt as she collapsed forward.

I mean it, I said. I think the two of us share a very special chemistry. And you're great in the sack.

She used the "f" word on me, which kind of ruined things. By then I had my thumbs in her throat. She began clawing at me, but I was a lot stronger and it didn't take long to kill her.

I felt the power.

I was just sorry it had to be Lorry.

# 54

---

I DUMPED HER IN THE MISSOURI RIVER WITH THE idea that she'd be carried to the bottom and that no one would find her body. To make sure, I tied the Mazda's heavy tire iron to her waist. I guess I didn't do such a great job of it because when her body hit the water I saw the rope come untied. The tire iron sank while Lorry floated on downriver with the current.

I'd botched the job. I'd been nervous and too hasty and I'd botched it.

I knew one thing: I had to get out of Great Falls. Fast. Before anybody found Lorry Haines.

I drove the Mazda out of town a few miles and left it in a wheat field. I couldn't keep driving it because I didn't know when Lorry's body would be found. When it was—when Lorry's picture was printed in the paper—Fred Farley would remember he'd sold her the Mazda and then the police would be looking for it. Better to be on the safe side and get rid of it early.

I mourned Lorry. I missed her. We'd had a really good relationship, the best of my life up to now. But I'd given in to the compulsion and killed her. I didn't want to do that. I wanted us to have a life together. But I went ahead and killed

177

her anyway.

Which meant I didn't have any real control left. None at all.

Lorry's death proved that.

# 55

---

WHEN PAUL VENTRY PHONED THE SHERIFF, ASKING
to see him immediately, Longbow picked up the call while
he was driving back from Crystal Lake in his Bronco. He'd
gone up there to interview an old fisherman named Charlie
Dobbs who claimed to have "direct personal information"
on how to contact the Big Sky Strangler. He wouldn't give it
over the phone. But he told Longbow he had it "all writ
down."

The trip had been worth zip—a totally wasted morning—
and Longbow was in an angry mood. Once the sheriff got
Dobbs to talk, the old man claimed that he'd had a vision
while he was fishing the lake. God came down from the sky
riding on a golden cloud. He was white-bearded, with blazing
eyes and a voice of thunder. ("I knew it was Him, all right,"
said Dobbs, "and He'd chose me for His messenger.") God
had told him how to contact the Strangler. He'd copied the
words down "direct from God's lips."

The note read: Contact the Big Sky Strangler c/o Santa
Claus at the North Pole, Alaska.

"Dang you, Charlie, you're crazier than ever," Longbow
told him, tearing up the slip of notepaper.

"If I am, it's all because a them pills the doc has got me
takin' for my bad liver," Dobbs had protested. "But I know
God when I see Him and I tellya He was out there on the
lake."

"You better have the doc recheck your prescription," Longbow had replied sourly.

Therefore, by the time he returned to Lewistown, the sheriff was in no mood to listen to ghost train stories from Paul Ventry, and told him so.

"I've collected some hard evidence," Ventry declared. "I need to see you right away."

"All right, all right," sighed Longbow. "But I got some shopping to do for the wife. You want to meet me at Russell's Market, I'll listen to you while I get the groceries. That suit you?"

Ventry said fine; he'd see the sheriff there in ten minutes.

Longbow hooked the cellular phone back in its cradle on the dash, allowing himself the luxury of self-pity. He wondered if the salary he got was worth his having to put up with so much crap.

Becky would say it was—but then his wife claimed he'd make a lousy storekeeper, which was what he'd set out to be. He'd wanted to run his own grain and feed store, but Becky swore he had no head for storekeeping. She'd been the one who'd talked him into running for sheriff.

And she was probably right.

She usually was.

# 56

RUSSELL'S WAS NOT CROWDED AND THE SHERIFF HAD managed to fill half a shopping cart by the time Paul Ventry approached him in the produce section.

"How's Becky doing?" the sheepman asked.

"Tolerable," replied the sheriff. "She's anxious to start walking again, but last time she saw Doc Kisner he said she's not to get off that couch except to go to the bathroom for at least another week. Seems this is a real critical time in foot surgery and the bones need to heal completely before she starts walking proper. So she's cranky as a wet bear. Sometimes I wonder why I ever married that woman."

"You don't mean that," said Ventry softly.

"No, I don't," admitted Longbow, ashamed of his insensitivity. "Becky's all I got."

Ventry looked around the produce section. "I'm not sure this is the best place to talk," he said.

"It'll be fine," said the sheriff. "You just show me what you've got that's so all-fired important it can't wait."

Longbow dropped several potatoes into a plastic sack, then moved toward the onions.

"I've been spending a lot of time at the library," said the rancher.

"Yeah. So I've been told." Longbow grinned. "Not much goes on around here that I don't know about."

"Then what do you know about these?" Ventry handed

the sheriff several Xeroxed news accounts dealing with local disappearances:

## NEWLYWEDS VANISH
### Fail to Return from Honeymoon

## TEENAGER MISSING
### Last Seen at Lewistown Depot

## MINISTER'S SON DISAPPEARS
### Victim of Possible Kidnapping

Longbow scanned the newsclips. "Well, I recall these folks were all reported as missing over the past few years." He handed back the articles, sacked a tomato and a head of lettuce and began pushing his cart toward the canned fruit section. "Too late for fresh peaches," he said, "so Becky told me to pick up two cans. Me, I can't stand canned peaches."

Ventry's tone was intense. "What did you do about these missing people?"

*"Do?"* The sheriff looked at him. "I ran a search for a couple of 'em. The others didn't rate one since it figured that they just got itchy feet and lit out."

"Were you aware that four of them were traveling by rail?"

"If I was, it didn't mean anything to me at the time," said the sheriff.

He selected two big cans of sliced peaches, a can of apricots and a can of pears, and dropped them into the shopping cart.

Ventry continued: "Several others were last seen in the *vicinity* of railroad tracks, in the general area bordering the Little Belt. The pattern is clear."

Longbow stopped his cart to face Ventry. "Mostly, these people were *young*, right?"

"Yes, but—"

"Young people leave home for a lot of reasons. They just take off and tell nobody where they're going. Then they get listed as 'missing persons.' But what happened is they just ran off to live their own lives. They usually turn up later, but the papers never write up that part."

"The way Amy has turned up?"

"I'm real sorry about your daughter, and I've near busted my ass trying to find her. But she's a special case. There's nothing to connect her to these others."

The sheepman's face was flushed. "But I've just *made* the connection. The *train.*"

The sheriff lowered his head. "Don't start all this again, Paul."

"You refuse to acknowledge the pattern?"

"There's *no damn pattern*! It's just in your mind. You're bending things all haywire to fit your ideas."

"The hell I am!" growled Ventry. "You won't listen to what I have to say because it falls outside the norm."

Longbow sighed. "All right, I'll listen. Tell me what you figure is going on."

"I'm convinced that all these missing people were murdered—including my daughter," said Ventry.

"And who's doing all the murdering?"

"A madman, living somewhere in the Little Belt. A freak rail buff, rich enough to buy an old steam train, restore it, and use it as a lure for his victims."

"If somebody was operating a private train in this area, I'd know about it."

"He's real clever. Only runs it in darkness, stopping at remote stations off the main line—like Bitterroot. Never runs the train by daylight. Probably keeps it up in the mountains. Uses off-line spur tracks. Comes rolling into a small depot late at night, between the regular passenger trains, picks up whoever's on the platform, then kills them once they're on board."

"And that's it? That's your whole theory?" The sheriff's eyes were tight on Ventry's face.

"Not all of it," said the rancher. "There's a definite *cycle* to these disappearances. According to what I've put together, the train makes its runs at specific intervals. About a month apart, spring through fall."

"And where is it the rest of the time?"

"Like I said—hidden away in the Little Belt. Maybe up in one of the old mine shafts. On an abandoned spur track."

"Are you finished?"

"No. I've done a lot of calculation on this, and I'm certain that the train will make its final runs during late October, into early November—before winter snow covers the tracks. Which means you've still got time to catch it."

"I can appreciate all the work and research you've put in," said the sheriff. "But you've built up this whole thing out of sheer speculation. It's absolutely natural that you're upset over your daughter, especially after losing Sarah and all, but dammit, Paul, this train is a fantasy that you've turned into a personal obsession. Go back to sheep ranching and try to resign yourself to the fact that Amy's gone. She's not coming back. And there's nothing you can do about it."

Ventry's jaw was set; his eyes burned with inner fire. "You'll see," he said. "You'll damn well see what I can do about it."

And he stalked out of the store.

# 57

JOURNAL: Thursday, September 27

     I WAS WALKING HIGHWAY 87, LOOKING FOR A RIDE.
I didn't have bus fare—which meant I had to hitch again. I
should have taken whatever money Lorry had in her purse,
but I never even thought of it. I had so much on my mind at
the time, getting rid of her body, making sure nobody spotted
me dumping her in the river and all that. I just left the purse
lying somewhere on the ground. That was dumb, too. Nothing I'd done had been properly thought out. Stupid.

     I was heading for Lewistown. There wasn't anyplace better
to go to and I had to keep moving. But when I got there, I
knew I'd have to sit down and really plan what to do next.
Things were heating up for me in Montana and—one way or
another—I'd be connected to a fresh murder. The Big Sky
Strangler would, anyhow.

     Whatever karma I had to work out here was sure not on
the positive side. The whole situation was negative and I was
getting really depressed.

     A blue Ford Probe stopped for me. I hustled over and
jumped in next to a short-haired guy, maybe 40 or so, in dark
green sunglasses. He was wearing tan slacks and a button-
down shirt under a brown jacket.

     How far you going? he asked me.

     Lewistown, I said.

Okay, I'm passing right through there. I'll take you the whole way.

Great. I appreciate the ride.

He got the Probe rolling along 87, not looking at me, keeping his eyes on the road. The scenery was as spectacular as ever, but I was not interested. I just kept staring down at my hands again, as if they had a life of their own and *they* had killed Lorry. Like that old horror movie, *The Crawling Hands* or whatever.

Heard the latest news? the driver asked.

No, I said.

Looks like the Big Sky killer pulled off another one.

He nodded toward the rear seat, toward a newspaper. I picked it up and scanned the headline story:

## MONTANA MANIAC STRIKES AGAIN
### Woman's Purse Leads to Body in River

How do they know this is the same guy? I asked. It could be a copycat killer.

That's possible, he admitted.

Guess this guy is proving pretty hard to catch, I said.

Murderers leave clues, he said. But a serial killing is tough to trace. There's usually not any obvious motive. In a family murder or a vengeance killing you've got a motive. You can start from there. But the serial killer just does his thing and moves on. Hard to trace.

The newspapers make a lot of stuff up, I said. You can't trust them to give you the truth about anything.

So you don't think the same killer is involved in this latest murder? he asked, eyes still on the road.

I don't know, I said. But it *could* be a copycat killer. Or maybe even a gang. They find a woman alone at night, attack her, and shove her in the river.

The purse still had her money in it, the guy in sunglasses said. If it was a gang of punks, they'd have taken the cash.

Yeah, I guess so, I said.

If the papers are right, about this being the same killer, then he's gotta be some kind of *animal,* the guy said.

I glared at him. You mean, because he—

He goes around strangling people! Just like that freak in Boston they made the movie about.

That was Albert DeSalvo, I said. And there's a big difference. DeSalvo was crazy.

Sure he was. *Anybody* who strangles people is crazy.

Not necessarily, I argued.

A nut is a nut, he said.

I was getting angry. I took in a deep breath. I had to be careful of going too far, of tipping my hand. I had to keep control of myself.

Maybe you're right, I said.

There's only one way to deal with a psychopathic killer, said the driver. You blow his lousy damn head off. That's how you deal with him.

And he let the flap of his coat fall back to show me the gun under his left armpit. A short-barrel .38 in a clamshell holster. I stared at it.

You look sick, he said with a grin.

I don't like guns, I said. Bullets can rip you apart, tear you to pieces inside.

Right, nodded the driver. And I've torn up a few scumbags with this little baby. And he patted the butt of the gun.

I'm a cop, he said.

I tried to act calm and cool, but I was badly shaken. And confused. Maybe, from the start, this guy had been baiting me. Maybe he had me tagged as the Big Sky killer from the minute I got into his car. My heart was beating fast and I could feel my cheeks tingling with heat as blood rushed through them.

You being a cop and all, I said, I guess you've actually seen what evidence the police have on the killer?

He grinned, nodded. Hey, not everything gets into the papers, he said. We got more than we're willing to share with John Q. Public. I've seen enough. I know he's in Montana, maybe even on this highway.

Then he slowed the car, easing it to the right shoulder of the road. He turned toward me, taking off the dark sunglasses. His eyes were hard and edged, like pieces of Montana granite. Cop's eyes. He held out his right hand. Show me some I.D., he said.

Sure, I said. I dug out my wallet.

I handed him a Florida driver's license. It wasn't mine. I never give my real name to cops. But this one had my picture on it and looked okay. I'd paid good money for it.

So you're Edward Jerome Conner, he said, reading aloud. From Miami. Home address on East Orange Avenue. He raised his cop's eyes to me. You're a long way from home, Eddie.

Vacation, I said. Then I grinned sheepishly. That's not quite the truth.

What is? he said. His granite eyes didn't blink.

The truth is, I've been out of work for awhile. I do odd jobs. Carpenter stuff, mostly. I take whatever comes along to make a buck. But things have been lousy in Miami, so I took what money I had—enough for a bus to Montana—to see Angie. She's my sister. But I ran out of cash, so I'm hitching the rest of the way in.

You gonna hustle your sis for some bread?

Oh, no. No way. She says she's already got some jobs lined up for me in Lewistown. I can start work as soon as I get in.

There was a moment when neither of us said anything. He kept looking steadily at me. Then he handed back the driver's license, put his glasses back on, and started the car.

We moved out onto the highway, running smooth again.

You nervous, Eddie? he asked me.

You bet. You got me shook real good with all this talk about the Big Sky killer. Showing me that gun you carry. For a minute, I thought *you* were him. But I guess he doesn't use a gun on people.

Sorry, the cop said. Didn't mean to shake you up, but I had to check. Just to make sure. You can't be the guy we're after.

Why do you say that? (I couldn't resist the question.)

I read people, Eddie. That's what I'm trained to do and I'm damn good at it. I can always spot a looney, just by looking into his eyes. And you're no looney.

Thanks, I said.

You like to fish? he asked me.

Used to. Haven't done any since I was a kid, I said.

Me, I love to fish. Every year, in the summer, I take off a

month and go trout fishing in Colorado. Kind of silly, I suppose, when there's such good trout right here in Montana. But I like the change of scenery. If I lived in Colorado, I guess I'd come to Montana to do my fishing.

That makes sense, I said. Everybody needs a change.

We drove along in silence. Then he said something that really threw me.

I'd like to meet your sister.

I had to swallow hard before I could respond. It was way out of left field.

She's . . . uh . . . too sick to meet people. I mean, she's bedridden. She's real sick.

What's the problem?

Cancer.

Bad? he said.

Real bad. She got it about three years ago. It's eaten her down to almost nothing. Doctor says she probably won't live out the year. That's one of the reasons I wanted to come to Montana. To see her one last time, you know.

The more I spun out the cancer story, the better it sounded. And he was nodding, buying it.

Cancer's a terrible thing, he said. I had a cousin die of it. Tough old buzzard. He fought it for five years, but it finally got him.

I guess it gets somebody in every family, I said.

Yeah. How old is your sister?

She's . . . thirty.

Got any other sisters or brothers?

Just my sis, just Annie.

Now he was pulling off the road again, slowing the car, stopping.

What's wrong? I asked.

Funny sound in the engine, he said. Pull the hood latch, will you, while I get out and have a look.

I slid over and pulled the handle under the dash and he raised the hood. I heard tinkering sounds.

Can you come out and give me a hand, Eddie?

Sure, I said. Be right there.

When I stepped around the edge of the hood he had his .38 out. Pointed at me.

What's the idea?

The idea is, Eddie, I think I've gone and netted me the biggest fish in Montana. But I was right about your eyes. You don't *look* like a looney.

Hey! You've made a big mistake if you think—

Details, Eddie. Details. That's how a cop puts things together. Like the first time you talked about your sister her name was Angie. Last time, you called her Annie. See what I mean?

Annie's her nickname. There's nothing strange about that.

Maybe. But you also told me you were hitching out to see her to get a job, not to pay her a final visit before she dies. You didn't mention anything about cancer until later.

I didn't argue with him. I just acted. It was my life or his.

I slammed the car hood down on his gun hand. Then I banged his head against the side of the Ford. He went down on his back, taken completely by surprise. He just didn't expect me to move that fast or do the things I did. I got the hood up while he was on the ground and pulled the gun free. I swung it toward him as he got to one knee.

And shot him four times. Pop. Pop. Pop. Pop. One right after another, like four loud handclaps.

The first bullet missed him, but the second took out his left eye. The other bullets hit him in the chest and the lower stomach.

He fell straight back and didn't move.

I leaned against the car and vomited. It was the first time I'd ever fired a gun.

I was about to toss it into the brush when I hesitated, looking down at it. I'd better hang onto the gun.

Just in case.

There were woods. I dragged his body off the road and left it among the trees, but first I got his wallet and keys.

I'd been lucky. No other cars had passed us while we were stopped. I slid back into the blue Ford and drove away without anyone seeing me.

A voice inside my head kept drumming four words, over and over: You killed a cop. You killed a cop. You killed a cop. You killed a cop.

# 58

AFTER HIS TALK WITH THE SHERIFF, PAUL VENTRY returned to the ranch and retired to his bedroom. He didn't want to face Josh and report how the meeting had affected him. Of how desperate and uncertain he felt. Ventry had told Longbow that he intended to *do* something about Amy's murder (and murder it was, without question), yet he had no plan of action, no idea now of where to go.

If only he could talk to Sarrie! She would have understood.

Ventry recalled the scene from the old John Wayne Western where Wayne goes out to his wife's grave and talks to her about his problems. He'd always considered the scene to be hopelessly sentimental—but now he wasn't so sure. Maybe *he* could do the same thing.

Now.

Here in this room.

Ventry sat down on the edge of the big double bed, his head lowered. "Sarrie, honey . . ." he began slowly, his voice soft and hesitant. "I don't know if you can hear me or not, but I need to say a few things to you."

He rose from the bed and walked over to the wooden rocker by the window, the one his wife had loved sitting in to watch the end of the day. Sarah had always found fresh beauty in the sunset sky, in the massive sweep of clouds stained orange and crimson by the retreating sun.

Ventry put his hand on the arm of the rocker, gently strok-

191

ing the smooth-grained wood. "Nobody believes me," he said. "Nobody wants to listen to me the way you used to listen. Even when I was dead wrong and you knew it, you'd hear me out, try to understand. Now nobody understands me. They keep telling me the steamer doesn't exist, that Amy never boarded it . . . never . . . died on it."

He turned from the window to slam his fist against the bedroom wall. "Dammit, Sarrie, I *know* I'm right and they're all wrong. You'd believe me. If you were here with me . . ." He paused, the words tight in his throat. ". . . we could face this together, find a way to make other people see the truth."

He looked at the empty rocking chair with agonized eyes. "You'd help me solve this thing. I know you would. I could always depend on you, Sarrie. Now . . . there's nobody." His voice had fallen to a whisper. "I've got nobody." He sighed, a deep, racking breath. "And I don't know what to do."

Beyond the Ventry ranch, the westward slanting sun cast long shadows across the length of Big Moccasin.

The day's end was near.

# 59

JOURNAL, continued:

    I'M BEING HIT WITH SOME REALLY BAD KARMA. Things just seem to keep getting worse.

I needed a car to get out of the state. Not the cop's blue Ford Probe. I knew I couldn't keep driving a dead cop's car, so I was on the lookout for another I could switch over to. I also needed a big chunk of cash to carry me for the next month or so.

I didn't think it would be such a hot idea to try earning money by getting a job in the area. Not with me looking so much like that composite drawing the cops are spreading all over the place. It's obvious that I need to hole up somewhere for a while until I can figure a way out of all this.

I got to thinking about stealing a Cadillac. I've always loved Caddies, the sleek way they look and drive. A Cad has real class. In my opinion, there's just no other car that can compare with it.

I continued towards Lewistown in the Probe, thinking about Cadillacs and how I could get one right now, when I remembered this book I read when I was a kid. It was about famous cars, and I really was impressed with the part which told about Al Capone's special Cadillac.

"Scarface Al," as they called him back in Chicago when

193

he practically ran the town, ordered up this custom 1930 V-16 Caddie and had it built to his own specifications.

They had pictures of it in the book. There were little portholes in the side windows so the passengers could stick their submachine guns out and blast away at Big Al's enemies or at people he wanted knocked off.

And if somebody tried to chase Al's car, there was this trapdoor through the floorboard where you could pour roofing nails down into the street to blow the tires on the cars coming up behind you. There was also a pressure can with a tube to add oil to the exhaust for a smokescreen.

Al had them put bulletproof glass in the windshield and side windows. And the driver's compartment was lined with quarter-inch armor plating.

All this made the car pretty heavy, so Al had them install a 16-cylinder, high-compression engine that could zip the Caddie along at speeds up to 120.

Yeah, that was *some* car. Al Capone always knew how to go after the best in life and even though he was a very dangerous and corrupt individual, I do have to admire his taste in automobiles.

So this sudden strong desire I had to steal me a Cad just sort of overrode my basic good sense. I realize that when you're trying to keep a low profile, you don't go around in a stolen Cadillac.

But there was a second reason I wanted to go after this particular make of automobile. I knew the person inside it would very likely be carrying a good amount of cash. People who drive Caddies are almost always loaded—so I'd be killing two birds with one stone as they say. I'd have a really classy getaway car and also the money I needed in order to hole up for awhile.

So I decided to do it.

I drove around the outskirts of Lewistown until I spotted this guy in a white Cad. He was driving all alone and it was dark by then, which helped the situation so far as I was concerned.

I waited for my chance, when just our two cars were going down a side street where there was no other traffic around. We were coming up to an intersection and when he began to brake for the stop sign, I drove right in front of him, forcing him into the curb.

He jumped out of the Cad all red-faced with his fists clenched. You stupid idiot, he yelled at me. You could have got us both killed!

No, I told him, only *one* of us dies.

And I went for his throat.

He was stronger than I'd figured and his blood was up, so strangling him was more of a problem than it usually is, but I banged his head back against the roof of the Cad, stunning him, and then I was able to do him okay.

There was some red mixed in with the silver in his hair. I guess he cut his head on the roof, but he was suffering no pain, being dead by then, so I didn't feel bad about having to bash his skull a little to get him calmed down.

The street was still totally deserted and I didn't see lights go on in any of the houses so I figured no one had seen what happened.

I got his wallet out of his coat and, sure enough, he had a whole bunch of hundred dollar bills in it. At the time, I didn't bother to count how many. (Actually, the total money I got from him was two thousand one hundred thirteen dollars, plus the dollar eighty-seven cents he had in change in his pants pocket.)

His driver's license said his name was Mitchell. Blair Edward Mitchell. There were business cards. He was President of the Mitchell Mining Company.

Hey, your middle name is *my* name, I said to his corpse. Anybody ever call you Eddie?

And I chuckled as I got his car keys and hopped behind the wheel of the big white Cad. *My* big white Cad!

Then I felt some panic. I was thinking that I'd better take his body with me and stash it somewhere. But that wouldn't solve all my problems because even if I took him with me, I'd still have to leave the dead cop's Ford there in the street. I couldn't get rid of the body *and* the Ford.

So I asked myself, why bother taking this guy along and maybe get spotted dragging him into the Caddie?

Just burn some rubber and get out of Lewistown fast.

Which is what I did.

I'm now sitting here in the white Cadillac. I've got the dome light on so I can write in my journal. I was hoping that writing would make me feel better, because there's a sense of desperation settling over me.

I can hardly breathe. My heart pounds as if it's going to leap right out of my chest. I feel as if a black hood has been pulled over my head. I am trapped inside myself and I don't know what to do.

I hate Montana.

My time here has been nightmare time.

I can't drive out of the state now. Every cop in Montana is going to be looking for Blair Mitchell's white Cadillac.

What I'm going to do is drive up into the Little Belt mountains, into the wilderness part, and stay there for at least a month. I can buy enough food at a supermarket to last me for that long.

Then I'm going to figure out what to do next.

# 60

"HELLO, MISS MITCHELL?"

"Yes."

"This is Sheriff Longbow. Afraid I've got some bad news."

"About what?"

"Your father. His Cadillac was stolen last night."

"So the insurance company buys him another. Is that your bad news?"

"No, ma'am, it isn't. The person who stole your father's car . . . well, there was a struggle . . ."

"Is my father hurt?"

"No, ma'am. He's dead."

## 61

BLAIR MITCHELL'S FUNERAL WAS A MAJOR EVENT in Lewistown. A huge number of people turned out for the occasion, filling every pew of the Lewistown Congregational Church—the town's biggest—and spilling over to the sidewalks which surrounded the large brick structure.

Despite the fact that his mining operation was unpopular with local environmentalists, Blair Mitchell's shrewd public relations plan now paid rich dividends. Reverend Harold McKinney lauded him as "a public benefactor . . . a fortunate man who cared for those who were less fortunate . . . a man whose countless acts of charity brought light into the community, creating joy and hope for the citizens of Lewistown, Fergus County, and all of north central Montana."

At the burial site, after his ornate brass-fitted coffin had been lowered into the ground and the final prayers had been said, Cris Mitchell broke down completely.

Her Aunt Jean, Blair Mitchell's younger sister, who had flown in from Florida for the services, now rocked Cris in her arms as the young woman sobbed out her grief.

"Your father and I saw life from quite different perspectives," said the older woman, "but I suppose at heart he was a good man with some very wrong ideas. We could never seem to agree on anything." She sighed. "He was far too ambitious and as stubborn as a mule—and if your mother were alive, believe me, she'd agree. They never got along either.''

Cris raised her tear-stained face, drawing back in anger, frowning at her aunt's words.

''Are you still harping on what was wrong with Dad? On *today,* of all days? My God, he was just put into the ground and here you are still criticizing him!''

''I have the right to speak my mind,'' declared her aunt.

''Not here, you don't. Not today. And not to me.''

Cris turned away, walking quickly, as the older woman stared after her.

''She's just like her father,'' murmured Jean Mitchell. ''Just like him.''

# 62

JOURNAL: Thursday, October 18

LIFE UP HERE IN THE MOUNTAINS HAS CALMED ME down a lot, eased my soul you might say.

I'm living in one of the old ghost towns. I don't know what they call this place. Not much left of it. Most of the walls have caved in or fallen over—and there isn't a sign around anywhere to tell me what the town was called.

What *is* left standing is the jail—they made it out of brick instead of wood siding—and I've been living in it for the last couple of days. I find this really ironic. I mean, I've never been put in a jail for anything in my life, yet here I am, living in one!

Ironic.

Found me a nice gold locket near some old spur tracks. Has an inscription on it. Belonged to some girl named Amy. I wonder, how did it get way up here?

I've got plenty of canned food. Enough for as long as I'm going to want to stay up here in the wilderness. Bought it at a little country store on the way up here with some of Blair Mitchell's money. I've had to decide not to become a vegetarian for awhile. Most of the cans have meat in them, like spaghetti and chili con carne and soup and stuff like that. I couldn't live just on canned fruit and vegetables—a person needs protein to be healthy, and up here I couldn't get food with enough protein unless I bought things that had meat in them. So I'll eat meat until I'm able to go down from the mountains and get out of Montana. When I do that, then I'll become a vegetarian. I've decided for sure. Good health comes first with me.

In a way, I like it up here. I can quit worrying about being a hunted animal. I was starting to feel like everybody was after me, before I came up to these mountains. And the compulsion seems like it's a million miles away. I don't even *think* about killing anyone and that's a wonderful blessing.

Maybe this is just what I needed to turn my life around. This period of peace and tranquility.

It's a real balm to my soul.

# 63

CRIS AND JOSH WERE EXTREMELY UNHAPPY. BOTH had been fully occupied with their separate crises during the past three weeks, with little time left over to be with each other. He'd been running the Ventry ranch, responsible for everything necessary to keep the place operating; she'd been immersed in the affairs of her father's businesses and the legal processes required by the various states which claimed jurisdiction over his estate. Blair Mitchell had been killed before he could carry out his plan to disinherit Cris, so she remained his sole heir and executor.

By mid-October the Mitchell legal situation, while still months away from resolution, was nevertheless under control. And Cris was more than anxious to resume her full-time relationship with Josh. With her father gone, she needed him more than ever. "If you'll meet me at Pepe's around seven, I'll buy you dinner," she told him on the phone.

"You've got a deal," he said. "See you at seven."

"You'd better bring your toothbrush," she told him. "You're going to need it tomorrow morning."

Pepe's West-Mex BBQ, Lewistown's only Mexican restaurant, was situated over a thousand miles north of the Mexican border. Pepe Sanchez, the establishment's founder, had been drawn from his native Sonora in Old Mexico eighty years earlier to work in the mines. When mining in the Little Belt went bust, he had no great desire to return to his ancestral home. Following immigrant tradition, he and his wife opened a Mexican restaurant on Main Street. Although Pepe's wife knew well how to prepare the traditional dishes, she faced supply problems in the restaurant kitchen. The cheese in Montana had to be bland American, the chile peppers had to be canned instead of fresh, and the masa had to be prepared from inferior American cornmeal. As it turned out, nothing served at Pepe's was quite authentic—but, thankfully, none of his Americano patrons ever knew the difference.

Pepe had died just as the local boys were returning home from Europe and the Pacific in the days following World War II. But his son took over the restaurant and, in turn, his grandson, who now had a five-year-old son of his own. Grandpa Pepe's hair had been jet black; continuous inter-marriage had lightened his great-grandson's to auburn-streaked brown, but after four generations the family bone structure was still Castilian-and-Aztec, as could be seen by anyone in the restaurant as the youngest Pepe, with typical five-year-old energy, was busily running from table to table while Cris and Josh tried to talk.

"I'm going to keep my promise," she told Josh.

"What promise?"

"I said that if I were in charge of Mitchell Mining, I'd shut down its operation in this area. Well, I'm now legally in control of the company, and as of next week, there will be no more mining in the Little Belt."

Josh let out a whoop. "That's wonderful! It's what we've all been working for. My God, I can't believe it's over."

"Believe it. It is. All over. You can ask my lawyer."

"Right now I feel like *kissing* your lawyer!"

"He wouldn't appreciate it." She grinned. "Try *me* instead."

And he kissed her.

Their lovemaking that night was tender and deeply passionate, and continued until the eastern horizon turned to pastel blues and pinks.

# 64

JOURNAL: Friday, October 19

IT GETS AWFULLY COLD UP HERE IN THE MOUNtains—below freezing every night—and I try to keep a fire going most of the time. Found an old pot-bellied iron stove in the ruins of what was once the General Store.

I've always been good with my hands (Ha! Didn't mean to be funny) and I got it set up and working pretty well. Found a rusted ax up here and sharpened it up some. Used it to cut wood for the stove. Once I get the wood burning, the old potbelly puts out a considerable amount of heat—so the nights up here aren't nearly as rough as they'd be without the stove.

Been doing a lot of daydreaming lately, about watching the trains go by down on the Kansas flats back when I was a kid. Guess being so near to all these old spur tracks got my mind working in that direction. Who knows? The human mind is like one of those Chinese puzzle boxes. You never know how to reach what's inside.

What I'm leading up to is that I had another nightmare— the first bad one for quite some time. I *hate* having these awful dreams, and I feel so weak and helpless when I'm caught up in them.

This one began with me somewhere down in Mexico (where I've never been in real life), walking over a landscape of dead trees and blackened rocks—like after an atomic blast.

I was alone and naked. I didn't seem to mind being naked in the dream, but let me tell you I would never go around like that when I'm awake. I don't believe in nude people. You know, the ones who go to some campground or beach or wherever and shuck all their clothes—where all these guys are walking around with their dicks hanging out for everybody to see. That's immoral, and it leads to pornography, which is one of the main things wrong with our society. I am proud to say that I have never, ever bought a pornographic book or magazine, and I have never gone to see a pornographic film. The only pornography I have had contact with was when sometimes I would see a centerfold of a naked woman that some guy had tacked up on the wall of an auto garage or something. And even when I was very close to a pornographic picture like that, I'm proud to say that I always looked in another direction so I never really saw it. I may have a problem with the compulsion, but I have never had a problem with pornography.

I'm getting off the subject of my nightmare. Anyway, I was walking naked through this blasted landscape and I stopped in front of a tree that looked like its head had been ripped off. It had two long clutching branches, like a pair of arms, and dead bark clinging to them like pieces of rotted black skin, and one of the long branch arms had a hand on it.

Like one of my hands.

A strangler's hand.

In this dream I was trembling, with saliva running down from my mouth—really terrified of this particular tree.

I knew it wanted to kill me.

The tree's dead hand closed over my neck. It tightened around my windpipe and I could feel the sharp-edged bark digging into my skin like razor blades.

I woke up choking and gasping for air. The wood inside the stove had burned down to ashes and the jail office (where I sleep each night) was cold as a tomb.

I got the fire going again, but I just couldn't get warm. Not until the morning sun came up.

Even then I was cold.

# 65

---

JOURNAL: Saturday, October 20

I'M LEAVING THE LITTLE BELT. GOING TO MAKE A run for it. Get out of Montana for good. And never come back.

I hate these mountains now. After what happened tonight I think I may be losing my mind up here, losing the ability to tell the difference from what's real and what isn't.

Maybe it's the solitude. It was great at first, but it gradually eats away at you, being alone in the wilderness. Maybe it's affecting the way I think, the way I see things. Or maybe it's just the pressure I'm under, with the whole state after me, everyone hating me for what the papers say I did. That could affect anybody.

But what happened to me tonight makes no sense, no logical sense at all.

There was a big yellow moon filling the sky and I was following one of the old spur tracks leading into the heart of the mountain, walking along the rusted rails thinking about the past, how it must have been back in the old days when the mining towns were going full blast, and the saloons were full of noise and laughter, with gaudy women in red silk dresses.

I was thinking what it would be like to just walk back in time, along these old rail tracks, to one of those mining towns and meet a fancy woman and how it would feel to strangle her and whether she'd be different from the women of today and how the skin of her throat would feel under my thumbs . . .

That's when I saw it. Around a bend of the tracks.

Something that shouldn't have been there, in this modern world, something from that distant past I'd been thinking about.

A steam train.

It was long and dark, just sitting there on the tracks, with its tall stack poking at the moon and its big iron engine looking huge and unreal in the night.

I was stunned. It just knocked me out. I mean, what the hell was an ancient steamer doing up here in the Little Belt? It belonged in some museum with the dinosaurs.

Then the really insane part began. The train seemed to be . . . *calling* me. Not in words, but from inside my head. I felt myself moving toward it; the train was pulling me in the way a magnet pulls in little black filings.

I stood next to one of the passenger cars, a long coach with dark windows like holes in a skull. There was a little metal step at the rear entrance to the coach and I was drawn to it. Despite my fear. And I was afraid, believe me. Plenty afraid. I knew that if I entered that coach I'd die. Just that simple. A clear feeling of awful dread for that dark train here in the middle of the Montana wilderness.

But I couldn't turn away!

I put my right foot on the boarding step . . . and suddenly I was . . . *rejected*. That's the only word that fits what happened. That force I'd been feeling, drawing me to the train, reversed itself. I was pushed back, violently, away from the coach.

*Evil repels evil!*

The words swirled in my head as I stumbled back, falling heavily onto the iced gravel by the side of the track.

Crazy thoughts filled my dazed mind. *You're tainted . . . tainted . . . tainted . . .*

I sat there gasping as the train, with a sudden burst of white steam, shuddered into motion, its big wheels grinding on the rails as it rolled away from me. Away.

Into darkness.

I didn't get up until the sounds of the steamer had melted and dissolved into mountain silence—leaving a ghostly residue of white steam in the air.

Somehow, I had been spared. I would have perished on that train. Don't ask me how I know, I just *know*. But it was my destiny to be spared.

Kathleen had been right about Montana. In karmic terms, I have faced death and transcended it. I have fulfilled her Montana prophecy. Death has passed me by.

Or am I going nuts? Did I even *see* the train? Was it all some illusion brought on by this wilderness life I've been living up here?

I'm not sure. But, in a way, I feel immortal.

And I'm no longer afraid of leaving the mountains.

# 66

---

It was a perfect fall day in the Little Belt; the trees blazed with color and the sky was vast and cloudless above the mountains, an inverted lake of blue.

Josh and Cris rode to the summit of Clear Creek Trail, high in the Belt, and stopped to water their horses.

"Sis and I used to ride up here when things got heavy at the ranch," said Josh. "It was one of Amy's favorite get-away places."

They sat at the edge of a small clearing surrounded by soaring pines. An unseasonably warm breeze stirred the branches, carrying the sweet scent of pine needles.

"It's a lovely spot," Cris said. "It does seem that we're really far away from everything up here—as if we're the only two people in the world."

"Just us and the mountains," Josh said. "You know, when the Indians lived up here, this was all sacred ground to them." He reached out to take her hand. "They'd appreciate what you've done—shutting down the mines, showing respect for the land."

"You're the one all these Indian ghosts should be thanking," laughed Cris. "*You* did it. Before I met you, I was blind. You opened my eyes to reality."

"I just pointed out some things," he told her. "You were the one with guts enough to change. Takes a lot of inner

209

strength to admit you're wrong. Most people just dig in their heels."

"What about Amy? Was she open to change?"

"Yeah," said Josh as he smiled in remembrance. "She was always willing to listen to other opinions. All of her pores were open, all the time. She was the most alive person I've ever known." He looked down, pulling at a tuft of grass. "It's hard to believe she's gone."

"What do you think happened to her?"

"I don't know." He shook his head sadly. "My dad believes some maniac on a steam train killed her. The sheriff thinks it was some road tramp—maybe even the Big Sky killer. I tend to agree with the sheriff. One thing I'm certain of—there's no lunatic rolling around central Montana in his own private steam train."

"Is that what your father *really* believes?"

"Yeah. Dad's obsessed with the idea. Like a dog with a bone, he just won't let go of it."

"You're seriously concerned about him, aren't you?"

"Damn right. He's been going deeper and deeper into this thing. He doesn't even *think* about the ranch anymore."

"What does the sheriff say?"

"He agrees with me that Dad is acting irrationally, that he's allowing his emotions about Amy's disappearance to cloud his judgment."

"Have you talked to your father?"

"I've tried. But it doesn't do any good. He doesn't really listen to me—or to anybody." Josh sighed. "God knows I miss Amy as much as he does. We were real close, always have been, even when we were little kids. But at least I can accept the fact that she's gone."

"I miss my dad, too," she said, her eyes misting. "It's funny, you know, I never thought I would. I loved him, of course. But he was always so fierce, so stubbornly sure of himself." She paused, thinking. "I used to get so mad at him I'd *wish* he were dead. Isn't that awful?"

Josh took her in his arms. "No, it's natural. You were just being human."

"I *did* love him, Josh. I just didn't know how much until

he wasn't around anymore.'' Tears welled in her eyes. ''Now I won't ever be able to tell him—he'll never know!''

Josh cradled her in his arms. ''He knows. You dad knows right now,'' he assured her.

''Do you think that whoever killed my father might be involved in Amy's disappearance?''

''It's possible. But that's up to Sheriff Longbow to find out.''

''I know,'' Cris said. She drew in a deep breath, sighing. ''It's so beautiful up here. I hate to go back.''

''Maybe you could turn yourself into a tree squirrel and stay up here,'' said Josh.

She smiled sadly. ''Except then I'd have to hibernate for the winter, and I have no intention of being away from you that long.''

He hugged her close as the breeze picked up. The trees moved fitfully as, around them, life stirred in the Little Belt.

*Unsleeping.*
*Hungry again.*
*Leaving its lair, to stalk the Montana plains.*
*Fiercely alive.*
*Confident in the power to entrap.*
*Screaming defiance into the vast night darkness.*

# 67

THAT NIGHT PAUL SLEPT WITH NEWT VENTRY'S Colt beside him on the night table. The last thing he saw before he finally drifted into sleep was a pale shimmer of moonlight outlining the weapon's long, blue-steel barrel.

At first he dreamed of brightly painted steam trains rushing along silver rails, of the sooty smoke from their stacks billowing up to darken the sky.

Darken.

Dark.

Black.

Moving black.

A train the color of midnight.

*The black death train!*

"Don't go near it," said a voice he instantly recognized. "Stay away from it, Paul!"

It was Sarrie. She was standing on the platform at Bitterroot station, her face a pale oval in the darkness, wearing her favorite blue dress, the one he'd selected for her burial. Her face was sunken, the lips wrinkled and bloodless. Looking as she had looked in the casket when he'd bent to kiss her cold face for the last time. She was between him and the black train, which waited silently for him.

"Stand aside," he told Sarrie. "I have to do this. I have to avenge Amy."

"It's impossible, Paul. Too dangerous." Her voice was tinged with dread and her eyes were beseeching, luminous under the stars. "Stay here with me. With *me*."

And suddenly she was young again, young and beautiful and radiant, exactly as she'd been when they'd first met and fallen in love.

She drew him into her arms. She smelled of spring flowers; her lips were full and quivering, her eyes like twin suns, hot and glowing.

They kissed passionately.

"Oh, Sarrie, how I love you!" said Ventry, holding her close, the soft mass of her hair against his cheek.

"Then you must do as I ask," she said. Her voice was young, a melody, sweet to his ear.

"I'll do anything for you, my darling," he said.

"Then stay with me. Don't go to the train. There's terrible danger for you!"

He looked beyond her to the night tracks. The black steamer loomed there.

Waiting.

He twisted away from Sarrie and started toward it.

"No!" she screamed.

She had Newt Ventry's Colt in her hand. Now she cocked it, aiming the gun at Paul.

"That's mine. Give it to me!" he yelled to her.

She fired. Again and again.

He felt the bullets rip into his body, tearing through his flesh; blood pulsed from his open mouth. He staggered, reaching for Sarrie . . . reaching . . .

And put his hand on the gun.

It was cold.

Sarrie was gone.

Paul Ventry was sitting up in bed, holding the bone-handled Colt tightly in both hands.

# 68

JOHN LONGBOW JAMMED HIS FOOT ON THE BRAKE
pedal and swung the Bronco around in a grinding U-turn.

He'd just seen Blair Mitchell's white Cadillac. No mistaking that car. Had an extra-long phone antenna on the trunk, plus those special mud guards for the back wheels. It was the stolen Cad and no mistake.

And it was moving fast, along State Highway 200, heading God knows where. He knew he could never catch up with it in a straight run, so he took a side road shortcut that would put him back on 200 ahead of the Cad—if he drove like a scalded bobcat, that is.

He made it, slamming the Bronco onto the highway just as the white car appeared in his rearview mirror.

Longbow unlocked the Remington pump from its seat stand and threw the Bronco across the road, jumping out.

He had the Bronco's red light going, but he knew that whoever was in that Cad wasn't about to pull over for a cop.

And he was right.

When Eddie Timmons saw the sheriff's car ahead of him, he floored the pedal and attempted to power around it.

Suddenly, a shower of glass exploded into his face, stunning him. Longbow had fired the Remington directly at the windshield of the Cadillac, shattering it instantly.

Eddie regained consciousness to discover that the Cad had

215

run off the highway into a roadside ditch. It was angled with the rear wheels in the air, still spinning.

He left the engine running as he pulled the dead cop's .38 from the glove compartment and threw open the driver's door.

Longbow was standing outside, facing him, holding the Remington. It was aimed at Eddie.

"Put down that fucking gun," the sheriff told him in a steady, cool voice. "If you don't, I'll blow the living shit out of you."

The lawman had a foul mouth and Eddie hated that. He thought he'd have time to trigger the .38 before the sheriff could act.

He didn't.

The Remington gouted fire.

And it was over.

Longbow found Amy Ventry's gold locket in the dead man's jacket. He checked a composite police drawing of Montana's most notorious criminal against the dead man. Jackpot!

"Son of a gun," sighed John Longbow. "I've gone an' bagged me the Big Sky Strangler!"

As soon as he got back to the office, the sheriff put in a call to Paul Ventry. But he refused to believe what Longbow was telling him—that his daughter had been a victim of Montana's serial killer.

"No," said Ventry. "He never strangled Amy."

"The hell he didn't!" fumed Longbow. "I found her locket in his jacket. The gold one—with her name engraved inside."

"I don't know where he got it," said Paul Ventry. "But that man had nothing to do with Amy's death. She died on the train."

"Oh, Christ, not that damn train nonsense again!"

"Not nonsense, John. *Truth.*" Paul Ventry drew in a breath. "The train exists. And I'm going to find it."

And he ended the call.

# 69

---

"HELLO, STEVE?"

"Yeah?"

"Paul Ventry. How you doing?"

"Fair to middlin', I guess. My back's been acting up again, but nothing serious. You?"

"I need to ask a favor," Ventry said, ignoring the question.

Steve Cavanaugh grunted at the other end of the line. "What kind of favor?"

"I need to fly over the Little Belt. Up near the summit. I was hoping you'd take me."

"Sure. Be glad to. A mountain flyover's no problem."

"Can we go early tomorrow, just after first light?"

Cavanaugh agreed. "Be at my place by sunup and I'll have the chopper gassed and ready to go."

"I'll be there," said Paul Ventry.

# 70

HE HATED HELICOPTERS. NOT ONLY HATED THE WAY they scared the sheep, but for another, more personal reason. His brother's son, Tom Ventry, had been permanently crippled when the copter he was flying crashed in Vietnam. The big Army chopper's main rotor blade had failed and the craft had gone down hard in a rice paddy. The crash had severed Tom's spinal cord, putting him in a wheelchair for life. He'd made the family proud—graduating from college, then going on to earn his doctorate in psychology after he got back to the States—but nothing would ever make up for what he'd lost. And it was all due to a damn helicopter.

Paul Ventry dreaded this early morning flight. He was nervous and uncomfortable sitting next to Cavanaugh inside the curving plastic nose bubble. The sun flared against their eyes as they flew east. As Cavanaugh swung the chopper around in a wide arc to head toward the rising bulk of the Little Belt Mountains, the sun dropped behind them. The loudly beating *whap-whap-whap* of the rotors intensified as speed was increased, but Ventry's throat mike and earphones kept him from having to shout.

"You didn't ask me why I wanted to make this flight," said Ventry.

"I figured you'd tell me in due course," said Steve Cavanaugh. He was a weather-roughened individual with the tough, blunt-fingered hands of an outdoorsman. His eyes squinted behind tinted glasses—and a full beard, raggedly trimmed, gave him the look of a man older than his forty-odd years. Cavanaugh was a dedicated sports buff; his leather flying jacket was set off by a sweat-darkened Chicago Cubs baseball cap.

"I'm looking for a train. On one of the old spur tracks," said Ventry.

"No trains in the Little Belt," Cavanaugh declared. "Not since the mines shut down."

"That's what everybody keeps telling me," said Ventry. "But this is a private train. A steamer. Runs down to the plains at night. Probably kept up here in a spur tunnel by day."

"You puttin' me on?" Cavanaugh asked, tugging at the brim of his cap. "Nobody runs steam trains these days."

"This guy does. A black steamer. I figure he keeps it up here in the Belt."

"You got any proof this train exists?"

"I don't need proof," said Ventry. "I'm convinced it does." His tone was sharp enough to warn off further questions from the pilot.

The Little Belt range now spread below them in a rich tapestry, from naked gray rock to multicolored trees and clumped sage—a terrain of aspen and lodgepole pine, spruce and fir, of textured granite and shale.

"If there *is* a train," said Cavanaugh, "I dunno how in hell you expect to find it. I can't set down in this kind of country. Too dangerous."

"I won't be asking you to do that," said Ventry.

"Well, then, if it's inside one of the old mine shafts, the only way you could check 'em would be on foot. And there's no roads left leading in."

"That's why we're in the air," stated Ventry, scanning the area below through a pair of binoculars. "I'm just hoping we might get lucky."

Admittedly, he told himself, the chances of spotting the black steamer were extremely remote. But perhaps he might catch sight of part of the train protruding from the mouth of one of the mine tunnels.

If so, he would find a way to reach it from the ground.

A slim possibility.

They flew over several abandoned mine tunnels with no success. Then . . .

"Wait!" Ventry shouted. "Down there to the left beyond the trees—on that spur track . . ." He adjusted the glasses. "I think I see it. Get lower."

He could make out a long, dark shape on the tracks. The black steamer?

The helicopter dipped lower, blades whipsawing the air.

"See it?" asked Ventry.

"I see something, but . . ."

"Damn!" exclaimed Ventry. "False alarm! It's just a fallen log."

In falling, the tree had stretched itself along the spur rails— an immense lodgepole pine, probably toppled by the mountain winds.

"It's time to wind up this little goose chase," said Cavanaugh. "I'm low on fuel."

"All right," sighed Ventry. "Let's head back."

The copter angled east, sliding down the blue arch of Montana sky, a shimmering metal bird, homeward bound.

# 71

AT THE RANCH THE FOLLOWING NIGHT JOSH AND his father shared a late dinner of canned beef stew, mashed potatoes, and apple pie from the bakery at Russell's Market.

Paul Ventry ate mechanically, his head lowered, silent throughout the meal. Finally, as they finished their pie, Josh expressed his sense of growing concern.

"Dad, this train obsession is destroying you."

Paul Ventry raised his head, staring at his son.

"Look at you," Josh continued. "You're like a robot. Nothing here at the ranch interests you anymore. We don't have talks like we used to. Hell, you won't even *argue* with me."

"There's nothing to argue about," said his father.

"You're letting this thing ruin your life."

"Man's daughter gets murdered, seems to me logical that his life *should* get ruined. What do you think I ought to do? Run for governor?"

"John Longbow is certain that Amy died at the hands of the Big Sky killer."

"Well, she didn't."

"How do you explain his having her locket?"

"I don't *have* to explain it. Makes no matter how he got it. They found out he'd been living up in the Belt. No doubt he found it up there—where the train took her."

"You went up in Steve Cavanaugh's chopper yesterday," said Josh. "Looking for that dream train."

"It's no dream—it's real," said the elder Ventry.

"No, Dad, it's *not*," Josh told him. "You're chasing a phantom and everybody knows it."

"I saw it, you didn't."

Josh slammed the table with his fist. "That was a *dream*, Dad! You saw it in a nightmare, caused by your grief over Amy."

"I had the dream before we knew she was missing."

"It doesn't matter. It still amounts to the same thing."

"Believe what you want," said Paul Ventry quietly.

"You need some help, Dad," said Josh.

"You mean a shrink?"

"Maybe a therapy group. For people who have gone through something like this. First Mom, and now Amy . . . it's too much for you. It would be too much for anybody." Josh hesitated. "I talked to Dr. McAndrews. He says there's a group that meets in Great Falls once a week. I'll go there with you . . . if you'll go."

"Why should I?"

"Because I care about you, that's why! Dammit, Dad, I *love* you."

Paul Ventry pushed back his plate, stood up, walked around the table and silently embraced his son.

# 72

MIDNIGHT.

Josh Ventry awakened with a gasp, sitting up abruptly in bed. Sweat beaded his upper lip and his hands were trembling. A feeling of terror, of cold dread, had drawn him up from sleep. His heart was pounding inside his chest and his skin tingled, as if an electrical shock had run through his body.

He switched on the table lamp next to his bed, pushed aside the covers and stood up, still shaky. The house was silent. Whatever had awakened him was inside his mind.

He put on his thick wool robe against the night chill and moved into the hall. His father's bedroom was at the far end, opposite the stairs, and Josh felt compelled to go there.

Something was wrong.

Very, very wrong.

He tapped on his father's door, got no response, and once again experienced a mounting sense of dread. He opened the door.

The room was unoccupied.

The bed had not been slept in. It was stark and white in the moonlight, reminding Josh of a satin-lined coffin.

He told himself not to be alarmed. Unable to sleep, his father was probably in the den, watching a late night movie on television. Or maybe in the kitchen, getting a snack. God knows, he'd not eaten much at dinner.

Josh hurriedly descended the stairs, illumined by the pale band of moonlight slanting in from the high windows.

He moved quickly to the den.

The room was dim and grave-quiet. No one there.

Josh was about to start for the kitchen when a white square of paper caught his eye. An envelope, propped against a book on the desk.

Josh ripped open the envelope, unfolding the handwritten note inside.

Josh—
I am going after the train.
Whoever runs it has to die.
I'll be back when this is over.
                              Love,
                              Dad

Numbly, Josh dropped his father's note on the desk. "Jesus!" he breathed.

Now, another thought suddenly propelled him to the hall closet. He opened the door, switched on the closet light and hastily stepped in, reaching toward the top shelf.

He removed an oilskin bundle from the shelf and unwrapped it to reveal a worn leather gunbelt and holster.

Several cartridges were missing from the belt.

And the holster was empty.

# 73

BY FIRST LIGHT PAUL VENTRY WAS DEEP INTO THE Little Belt, climbing steadily toward the summit of Moccasin Peak. He was riding Prince, his favorite stallion, a long-striding mountain veteran who seemed almost human to his master. Prince carried a blaze of white between his eyes and a white triangle on his chest. Otherwise, he was chestnut brown, his coat glistening like oiled leather on his sleek-muscled body.

In the saddle roll Ventry had food, blankets and rain gear, in case the storm that was brewing above him should hit the mountains. Also in the saddle roll: Newt Ventry's Colt revolver, with enough rounds to get the job done.

He was going to kill the man who kidnapped Amy. What Steve Cavanaugh didn't know—what no one knew—was that the chopper flight over the Little Belt had been successful. After spotting the fallen pine tree, bare seconds before the helicopter swung around to head back for Cavanaugh's ranch, Paul Ventry's binoculars had picked up a flash of dull metal at the mouth of the old Danvers Mine. As the chopper angled sharply past the spur rail leading into the mine, Ventry was able to see the projecting bulk of the train just inside the tunnel.

There was no mistake. It was the phantom steamer—the one from his dream, the same one Amy had boarded at Bitterroot station.

The black death train.

He was about to cry out to Cavanaugh—but had changed his mind. He'd made an instant decision: he would seek out the killer on his own and avenge his daughter. Cavanaugh must not know. Josh must not know. It was a solo task Paul Ventry had to accomplish, a private mission of vengeance that he must perform alone. He didn't want Sheriff Longbow sending his deputies to Moccasin Peak to do the job that must be his.

The train freak would die under his hand. He could see it happening clearly in his mind's eye—the wilderness confrontation between the two of them, the barrel of the big Colt coming up, the pressure on the trigger, the bullets smashing home, blasting the man's head apart, the killer falling, choking in his own blood . . .

Clear and vivid.

And satisfying.

However, as Ventry rode closer to the summit, questions began to assail him. What if the train was no longer there? Obviously, the Danvers Mine was its home base, the place chosen to shelter it between midnight runs down to the plains. The steamer would be kept there by day, he was sure of it. But could he be equally sure that the killer himself would be with the train? Perhaps not—but the chances were good that he lived *on* the steamer, or near it in the mountains. And if Ventry had to wait for him, then he was prepared to do just that.

But I don't think I'll have to wait, he assured himself. My gut tells me he's *there*—and all I have to do is find him and kill him.

From the night of the dream to this moment, Paul Ventry felt that he was destined to face this madman and destroy him.

He was fated to avenge Amy.

Reaching the mine was difficult. There were no longer any passable roads into the area and he couldn't simply follow the rail track in. If he tried that, he could be observed by the killer he was stalking. The terrain was confusing. He was using a map of the Little Belt which indicated the sites of the original silver and gold strikes, but pinpointing the exact location of the old Danvers Mine was no easy task. Things looked considerably different from the ground than from the air.

Ventry got lucky. Halfway to Moccasin Peak he found an ancient wooden sign, the letters badly chipped and faded, bearing the words DANVERS HILL. The name of a small cow town founded by Jedediah Danvers, the man who had struck gold in this area. The town had burned down in 1890, after a drunken fight during which the saloon had caught fire, and now nothing remained of the place. But Ventry knew that the mine was situated just a mile east of the town, so he must be close.

He allowed Prince to drink some fresh water from a clear running creek, then urged the big chestnut forward.

Ventry began picking his way more carefully now, staying within sight of the old rail line which climbed steadily upward.

Thick trees and heavy outcroppings of rock afforded him ample cover, but the incline was steep and treacherous. Occasionally, Prince would dislodge a loose bit of shale which clattered behind them, and Ventry worried about being heard, but he seriously doubted that his quarry expected an attack in these rugged mountains. And there were bears and other wild animals who foraged the woods, so the sound of dislodged rocks was normal here.

Closer now. Much closer. Ventry dismounted, leaving Prince tied to a young pine. He advanced cautiously on foot. Just ahead of him, through a screen of trees and heavy brush, he could make out the dark mouth of the mining tunnel.

And, just as he knew it would be, the black steamer was there.

The train from his dream. Motionless and silent in the warmth of late afternoon. He could recognize the rear section of the passenger coach—the one with Amy from his nightmare—protruding from the tunnel.

Ventry felt the surge of adrenaline in his body; his heart beat faster, his breath quickened. By God, he'd been right all the time; it was *true,* what he'd seen! The black steam train existed—as he had claimed from the beginning. If only John

Longbow could be here now. Ventry would savor the shock and surprise on the lawman's face.

No, it was better this way. He had to face the murderer alone; he wanted the deep personal satisfaction of pumping those bullets into the body of Amy's killer.

He was certain now that she had died on this train. The certainty lay as solid as a stone in his mind.

Ventry pulled the heavy Colt from the saddle roll, tightening his right hand around its yellowed grip.

Then he left the trees and moved quickly to the train.

Boarded it.

Inside, Paul Ventry was sure, he would find Amy's killer. Every fiber of his being told him that the killer was here.

*Here.*

Something slashed at him from the inked darkness. Razored teeth opened Ventry's left thigh and an incredible wave of pain swept through his lower body.

"Bastard!" shouted Ventry. "Where are you? I can't *see* you!"

Again. The teeth slashed at him again with a terrible ferocity.

He grunted, dropping the gun.

His right arm was opened to the bone and his right hand was numb, useless.

Ventry fell to his knees in the aisle, fumbling for the Colt with his left hand.

Something swept up at him.

"No!" screeched Paul Ventry.

It was the last sound he made as his head, at shoulder level, was severed from his body.

Then there was only blood.

# 74

PRINCE RETURNED TO THE VENTRY RANCH LATE THE next afternoon. The big stallion had managed to break his tie rope; when his master failed to appear, the horse had trotted home.

Josh was greatly concerned. He had no idea where his father had gone in pursuit of the black steamer, but he was certain it was a location somewhere in the Little Belt. Perhaps the horse had wandered back on his own, but there was a good chance that Paul Ventry had sent Prince back as a call for help. He could have fallen from the saddle somewhere in the mountains.

However, Josh reasoned, if this were the case, his father would have sent back word as to his location. There was no note of any kind in the stallion's saddlebag.

Josh immediately contacted the sheriff, who promised to mount a land-and-air search of the Little Belt. Since the area was so vast, the chances of spotting Ventry were slim—even if he were still alive.

"We'll find him," declared John Longbow. "Your daddy's tough. He'll survive."

Josh believed otherwise.

"I think he's dead," he told Cris. "I think he found the train and died on it—just like Amy." They sat on the wide wooden veranda steps as the shadows of late afternoon lengthened toward dusk. It would be dark soon. The deep Montana night was almost upon them.

"I argued like hell with Dad about his phantom steamer," said Josh. "Maybe if I'd listened to him he wouldn't have gone out alone the way he did. He might still be alive if I'd listened."

"How do you know he *isn't* still alive?" she asked. "He could have fallen in the mountains."

"Dad was an expert horseman. He didn't fall. The stallion's tie rope was broken. Prince did that after Dad left him. I *know* my father, Cris. If he were alive, Prince would never have returned without him."

"But what if your father was on foot and lost his way? Maybe he couldn't get back to the horse."

Josh shook his head. "Dad *knew* those mountains. He'd never get lost in the Little Belt. In my gut I'm certain he found that train—and died on it."

"The sheriff will never—"

"Damn the sheriff," snapped Josh. "He's got his mind made up. He can't help me do what I have to do."

His voice was low, intense, containing an uncharacteristic note of cold resolve that alarmed Cris. She didn't like what she was hearing.

"*What* do you have to do?" she asked.

"I have to finish what Dad started. I'm going after that fucking train!"

# 75

By the close of the following day, as the mountain search for Paul Ventry continued, Josh had reviewed all his father's papers dealing with the steam train. He had pored over the notes Paul Ventry had made at the Lewistown library relating to rail-associated disappearances in the area. The sun was vanishing behind the Little Belt, banding the walled bookshelves in shades of pale gold, as Josh pushed the last folder aside. He stood up, stretching tired muscles. There was an ache behind his eyes and his leg muscles were tight and cramped.

He was beginning to plan his action against the train when the phone rang.

Cris. Calling to apologize.

They had argued the previous evening. Josh had made his decision; Cris was unable to change his mind. She didn't want him to go on what she termed "a crazy vigilante mission." But Josh ignored her pleas. Finally, she had stormed away from the ranch in her van, tight-faced with anger.

"I'm sorry about last night," Cris said. "I really laid into you."

"I had it coming," he admitted. "Sometimes I can be as stubborn as Dad."

"Any word on him?"

"No, but I didn't expect any."

"You still intend to go out on your own?"

"Yep. I'm leaving tonight."

"For where? You don't know how to find the train."

"I'm gonna let it find me."

"But how?"

"If I tell you, will you swear not to tell the sheriff?"

"I swear."

"There's an abandoned rail depot called Ross Fork two miles beyond Bitterroot station—out on the central plains. I'm going to wait there for the train. When it shows up, I'll flag it down."

"How can you be sure it *will* show? Or when?"

"The weather's getting colder. We're due for snow any day now."

"So?"

"So the train will want to make as many kills as possible before the snow shuts down the spur lines into the Little Belt. It'll be running a lot after midnight, looking for passengers, and I'm going to be there at Ross Fork. I figure I won't need to wait more than a couple of nights at most."

"Okay," sighed Cris. "Let's say the train *does* come and let's say it stops for you. What will be waiting inside?"

"I wish I knew—but I think there's something more than a human being connected with it."

"What does that mean—more than a human being?"

"I don't know," Josh admitted, shaking his head slowly. "It's just a strong feeling I have—that whatever's on that train isn't just some rail freak on a killing binge." His eyes took on a hard shine. "*Whatever* it is, I'll be ready for it. I'm going to bring along explosives—blow that sucker apart! I can do it. I know I can."

"You mean, *we* can."

"Huh?"

"I'm going with you."

"Oh, no, you're not."

"Wrong, Josh. You *need* me."

"For what?"

"To blow up the damn train. *I'm* the explosives expert, remember?"

"This is going to be dangerous. I don't want you involved."

"Tough. I *am* involved. I'm involved in anything you do from here on. Besides . . ." Josh could hear her chuckle over the phone. "I know too much."

"What's that mean?"

"Means you told me exactly where you're going. If you don't take me along, I'll phone Sheriff Longbow and he'll go out there and stop you."

"But you swore you wouldn't tell him!"

"I lied."

"You'd do it, wouldn't you?"

"Damn right I would. I'm serious about this."

Josh pondered her words for a moment. Then he said, "All right. We go together."

# 76

THEIR PREPARATIONS WERE THOROUGH. THEY WORE extra-heavy work boots and thick leather gloves for better protection in case of a possible animal attack. Their clothing was layered against the night cold and each wore a sheepskin storm coat with a fleece-lined hood.

They were equally well-prepared with weapons. In a strap bag, Cris carried plastique explosive as well as a short-handled Woodsman ax. Josh took along a wide-bladed hunting knife in addition to his Winchester pump.

"You'd think we were getting ready for World War III," said Cris as Josh loaded extra ammunition into her van.

"No way to tell what we're going to be facing," he said. "Once we're on board the train, anything can happen. We don't know who or what will be waiting inside to kill us."

"You're really convinced of all this, aren't you?"

"I am now. For a long time I agreed with the sheriff—that it was just in Dad's head. But after going through his notes and papers—and with him disappearing the way he has—there's no question he was onto something."

"But you can't be sure of exactly what."

"I'm sure the train exists—and I'm convinced Amy died on it. And Dad, too, most likely. That's enough for me."

"Okay," she said with a nervous smile. "I guess we're ready to leave."

"Not quite," he said, taking Cris into his arms, kissing her deeply.

*"Now* we're ready," he said.

A cold Montana night wind was lashing the plains when Josh and Cris arrived at Ross Fork. They parked her van behind the abandoned depot and moved to the wooden platform facing the tracks.

"Watch your step or you'll go right through these boards," warned Josh. "They're pretty well rotted out."

Cris nodded, stopping to peer inside the small depot through the shattered front window. A few shards of broken glass still clung to the weathered frame. Cris shivered from a knifing gust of wind and pulled the hood of her coat closer to her face.

"If we went inside we'd be a lot warmer," she said.

"Sure we would," agreed Josh. "But we want whoever's on that train to see us out here on the platform. If the steamer doesn't come tonight, we'll spend tomorrow inside."

"Okay," she nodded. "I'm willing to freeze my butt off if you are."

Cris was trying for lightness, using humor to mask her fear. She was nervous and tense as she thought about the grim battle ahead. If the train *did* stop for them, what dangers would they face in trying to destroy it?

This whole situation was bizarre, surreal—the two of them out here in the middle of the Montana plains waiting to do battle against a phantom steamer! Only her deep love and concern for Josh kept her from jumping into the van and driving away from Ross Fork. It was incredible what they planned to do; it touched on the irrational. There was still no *proof* that anything Josh believed—or that his father had believed—was actually true. For that matter, Cris was still not entirely convinced the phantom steam train truly existed—and waiting for it here, in the bitter cold of a wind-whipped night, seemed an act of madness.

She huddled next to Josh on the platform's single wooden bench, pressing into his body for warmth—and because she felt less afraid, less uncertain, when she was physically close to him.

"I still don't understand why no one reported seeing the train," she said. "I mean, a steamer would attract a lot of attention."

"Only by daylight," said Josh. "And only if it ran through populated areas. But this one runs after midnight out here on the plains. The people who do see the train don't live to talk about it."

"It's hard to believe all this," she told him. "I keep trying, but—"

"Hey!" He tipped up her chin with a gloved hand. "I was just as skeptical as you are until I went through Dad's papers."

"But you *wanted* to accept it by then," Cris said. "You wanted to support your father in his belief."

"Maybe I did," Josh declared. "But when a black steamer stops in front of this depot, you'll know I'm right."

"And what if it never comes?"

Josh looked down the track, past a rusting water tower to the silver rails vanishing into wind-gusted darkness.

"It'll come, Cris," he said softly. "It'll come."

# 77

THE TRAIN DID NOT ARRIVE THAT NIGHT.
Or the following night.

# 78

THEIR FOOD SUPPLY WAS EXHAUSTED AFTER THE second day and they had driven the van to the general store at Marler's Crossing for fresh supplies—cheese and bread, canned peaches and pears, apples and bananas, Cokes, and a large package of Trail Mix with sunflower seeds, raisins, and almonds.

Back on the platform with Cris, late into the third night as he spooned peaches from an open can, Josh attempted to convince himself anew that the black steamer would indeed roll into Ross Fork.

"We're on the direct line from Bitterroot," he told Cris. "It'll *have* to pass through here to reach a return track running back into the Little Belt."

"Fine," said Cris. "But what if it's not out looking for more victims?"

"It's bound to be. This would be close to its last chance for the season. According to the news clips Dad collected from the library, several of the disappearances all happened in a row—during the final weeks of fall, before the first snows. Whoever or whatever's on that train is a hunter, and it'll be out hunting as long as the weather holds."

The wind had ceased; the night was calm under a clear, diamond-dust sky. Cris finished off an apple, then flipped the tab on a Coke. She took a long swallow, then shook her head slowly.

"This isn't real, Josh . . . all because Amy *thought* she saw a steam train waiting for her, and your father *thought* he could find it in the mountains. There's no steamer," she said flatly. "There never was."

Josh said nothing. She was voicing his own doubts and he had no argument left to present. He checked his watch.

Five minutes to midnight.

The train came at midnight.

Josh sensed it out there in the ash-dark Montana night; he felt it in his blood and bones.

He sprang from the platform, unsnapping the long three-cell flash from his belt, running toward the glimmering silver tracks.

"Do you *see* it?" Cris shouted, scrambling after him as he knelt by the rails, pressing the cold metal.

"No, but I *feel* it," he said. He raised his gloved hand. *"Listen!"*

They could both hear it now, rushing toward Ross Fork, clattering in fierce-wheeled thunder, sliding over the rails like an immense, segmented snake, with its single yellow eye probing the terrain ahead.

The black train was in sight now, coming fast, its locomotive beam slicing a bright round hole in the darkness. Josh stepped to the center of the track and began swinging the flash. He had the Winchester strapped along his right side, under his long sheepskin coat. The knife at his belt was equally well hidden.

Cris stood beside him, fear rioting through her mind. The train really existed. Nightmare had become reality. Her gloved fingers touched the Woodsman ax inside the shoulder bag. Before the night was done her life might depend on this weapon.

"Keep behind me," Josh told her. "When it stops, I'll board first. You follow me. Okay?"

She nodded, her muscles tight with tension.

Now the rails were vibrating beneath him as Josh continued to swing the flash.

Bet it's surprised to see us, Josh thought. Two more ripe victims out here for the taking. A young couple alone at night. Easy prey.

Meat for the hunter.

Now the sweeping locomotive beam splashed their bodies with pale luminescence.

Ventry swept his flash up, then down, in a high arc. Again. And again.

Stop, you bastard! *Stop!*

The train began slowing.

Sparks showered from the massive driving wheels as the steamer reduced speed. Slowing . . . slower . . . steel shrieking against steel—an easing of bulked force, a reduction of primal energy.

It was almost upon them.

Like a monstrous shining insect, the locomotive towered high and black above them, its tall stack shutting out the stars. The rusted tip of the train's thrusting metal cowcatcher gently nudged the toe of Ventry's right boot as the incredible night mammoth slid to a final grinding stop.

Now the train was utterly motionless, breathing its white steam into the cold darkness—waiting for them as they had waited for it.

A red glow emanated from the steamer's interior. A door in the first passenger coach, directly behind the coal car, opened like a dark wound.

Inviting them in.

Josh clipped the flash to his belt, glancing back at Cris. Her face was pale and strained, but she nodded to him. She was ready.

Josh swung aboard, pulling her up behind him.

They entered the interior of the coach. Would a killer be there to meet them? Josh gripped the Winchester beneath his coat. You've had one surprise tonight, you son of a bitch! Get ready for another.

With a hissing sound, the coach door sealed itself behind them—and the steamer jolted into life. They were thrown to their knees as the train lurched violently forward. The locomotive's big driving wheels sparked against steel, gaining a solid grip on the rails as the black steamer surged powerfully away from Ross Fork.

They stood up now—gaining balance in the swaying coach. To either side, rows of richly upholstered green velvet seats lined the aisle, and a dozen ornate, scrolled gas lamps ran the length of the car. They cast flickering shadows over antique brass fittings on the hand-carved wood ceiling. Thick green brocade draped the windows.

Josh Ventry didn't know much about trains, but he was sure that this one *had* to be pre-1900. Beautifully restored . . . by whom?

The car was empty. They were alone.

Then, incredibly, viscid black bubbles began to form on the ceiling at the far end of the coach. Growing. Quivering. Multiplying.

"What's happening?" Cris gasped.

"I don't know," Josh told her. He stared in shock at the loathsome globes as they swelled and burst, releasing pulsing black, snakelike strands which writhed and thickened, taking on form.

Human form.

Men and women. Young and old. Moving toward Josh and Cris in the clicking interior of the coach with the relentless progress of figures from a dream, their coal-red eyes glowing hypnotically.

"Sweet Christ!" breathed Josh, as the advancing faces became suddenly clear to him. He'd seen photos of them in the news clips among his father's papers—the men and women reported missing in the plains area—and two of them were . . . were . . .

"It's Amy," he cried out. "And Dad!"

Instinctively, Josh dropped the Winchester and started forward.

"No!" screamed Cris. "Stay away from them!"

Amy had her arms extended toward her brother, and Paul Ventry was reaching out in order to grasp his son's hand. Their eyes glowed in the semidarkness.

Transfixed, Josh moved down the swaying coach aisle toward them as Cris scooped up the Winchester, pumped the weapon, and fired.

Amy's skull flew apart at the first blast, but the headless thing kept advancing. A second blast from the pump gun cut Paul Ventry in half at hip level—but his lower body continued to shamble forward with the others.

The double roar of the Winchester had roused Josh. Blinking dizzily, he fell back toward Cris. "My God, what *are* they?"

"Whatever they are, they're not alive," she said numbly. "Don't look in their eyes. If we don't look in their eyes, they can't hurt us."

As she said this, the nightmare figures began to waver, losing form, melting down in a black ooze into the aisle.

Again, Josh and Cris were alone in the swaying coach.

"I was right," he said softly. "There's no madman in here waiting to kill us. Nothing human could have sent those . . . those *things.*"

The floor of the coach suddenly rippled beneath their feet like the shuddering skin of an animal; then the movement ceased. The floor was solid again.

"What was *that*?" gasped Cris.

"Give me the ax," Josh said tightly.

Cris fumbled in her shoulder bag, handed the Woodsman to him.

Josh pivoted toward one of the upholstered aisle seats, raised the ax high and brought it down in a swift arc, sinking the razored blade deep into the green velvet seatback.

Black fluid gushed from the cushion and a rubbery mass of coil-like innards erupted from the wound like spilled guts— as the train's screaming whistle pierced the rushing darkness.

Josh stepped back, breathing fast. "Oh, sweet Jesus! It's alive! The whole fucking train is *alive*!"

Teeth were forming. Long and curved like the fangs of a cat, sprouting from the floor and ceiling in daggered rows.

Cris shrieked as the floor moved upward, while the ceiling, lined with teeth, began to descend. They were in the train-thing's mouth—and the jaws were closing on them. Josh had the Winchester now, and fired twice, blowing a gaping hole in the exit door. But instantly, with a thrashing movement, the edges of the hole closed as the wound sealed itself.

"We're trapped!" moaned Cris. A voice in her mind was screaming. *Can't be. Can't be. Can't be.*

"Here . . . take this . . ." Josh tossed the pump gun to her and attacked the platform exitway leading to the coal car with a series of savage ax blows, jamming his body into the wound before it could close.

The ceiling and floor were now only a few feet apart. The creature's fanged teeth ripped at Cris, drawing blood as they slashed through the shoulder of her coat. Crying out in pain, she dropped the Winchester, lurching toward Josh. With his body wedged in the gummy opening, he grabbed Cris at the exact moment the jaws of the train-thing snapped shut. The razored teeth chopped off the heel of her left boot as Josh dragged her through the opening. The ax slipped from his hand, clattering down onto the tracks.

Now they were crouched on the platform of the coal car, just behind the giant locomotive, buffeted by wind and blowing cinders as the death train roared along the rails.

"We can jump," shouted Cris.

Josh leaned close to her, his mouth to her ear. "Can't. Not at this speed."

But the train was slowing as it began its climb into the Little Belt.

"Now!" Cris nodded toward the ground. "We can make it now."

"*You* jump," Josh told her, taking the strap bag from her shoulder. "I have to stay."

"*Why?*" Her voice was agonized as her eyes searched his face.

"To kill it," Josh replied. He nodded toward the bag. "Blow it to pieces."

Cris understood. If they left the train now, it would escape them and go back into hiding deep within its mountain cave. Amy and Paul Ventry would not be avenged; the job they came to do would not be accomplished.

"I'm staying," she told him. "We do this together!"

He accepted, returning the shoulder bag without argument, knowing he needed Cris to set and time the explosive charge.

Again, he placed his mouth close to her ear. "You want to kill a snake, you cut off its head. We go for the brain." And he pointed toward the locomotive.

She nodded mutely.

As Josh worked his way around the outside of the coal car,

with Cris directly behind him, his mind grappled with the fact that the steamer was actually a living entity.

It's what the Indians talk about, he told himself, what they call a "spirit life." Ancient and rusting for more than a hundred years, on sacred ground in the high mountains, the train had slowly taken on a sentient life. The molecular components of iron and wood and steel had, over this slow century, transformed themselves into living tissue, achieving organic form.

And the dark hell-thing had rolled down onto the Montana plains seeking food, seeking blood and flesh to sustain it, sleeping, sated, through the frozen winters, hibernating, then stirring to hungry life again as the greening earth renewed itself . . .

They had reached the coal tender's outer platform; it gave beneath their boots like sponge. Josh knew they were very close to the train-thing's life source. The high sides of the car shielded them from the wind, making conversation possible.

"Do you think the train knows we intend to kill it?" asked Cris.

"It sure knows we're the enemy."

"Then . . . it's still dangerous."

"I'd say *damn* dangerous. We don't know what it's capable of—what powers it has. We already know it can generate ectoplasmic reproductions of its own victims."

"That's awful!" Cris shuddered.

"Time to move," said Josh.

They left the coal tender and scrambled up to the engine platform. Directly in front of them, blocking their view of the interior, a thick, gelatinous membrane stretched across the width of the locomotive. A curtain of alien flesh, pulsing with life.

"We've got to get through this to reach the brain," Josh told her.

"If we had the Winchester—"

"I think I can cut through it with this," he said, producing the wide-bladed hunting knife from his belt.

The flesh curtain rippled in fluid, repulsive movement as Josh attacked with the knife, driving the blade deep into the veined tissue.

Again, the train-thing screamed, the high-pitched shriek of its locomotive whistle filling the vast Montana night.

Josh tugged at the knife handle, drawing the blade downward to split the membrane like a swollen peach.

They ducked through the gap into . . .

*A horror.*

Brass and wood and iron had become throbbing flesh. Levers and controls and pressure gauges were coated with a thick, crawling slime; the roof and sides of the engine cab were heaving.

In the center of the cabin a red mass of tissue pulsed rhythmically, bathing the area in hellish crimson light. Pus-yellow ganglia shimmered across its surface.

A powerful stench, like rotting, overripe fruit, permeated the cabin and Cris fought back a rising nausea as she gripped Ventry's arm. She was trembling; every nerve in her body was assaulted by the living horror surrounding them. Her mind screamed: *Get out! Get out!*

But Cris controlled her panic. They had to destroy this thing; they had a job to finish.

With her eyes still fixed to the mass of glowing tissue, she dipped a hand into her shoulder bag and withdrew the explosive charge. It was no larger than a cigarette package, but its destructive power was awesome.

"We need to be clear of the area before I activate it," she said.

"All right," nodded Josh. "Let's do it and get the hell out."

The train reacted.

The entire cabin flowed into abrupt motion, heaving up in a bubbled, convulsing pincer movement, trapping them like flies in a web.

Cris twisted, screaming, within the jellied grip of the train-thing. The explosive device had been jarred from her grasp, lost in the bulk of crushing slime-tissue.

Josh plunged his right hand into the wormed mass, trying desperately to reach the device, but a host of needles ripped at his fingers. Instinctively, he pulled back. His right thumb was entirely bitten away!

"Teeth!" he declared in numb shock. "It's . . . eating us alive."

Cris felt lancing pain as a row of fangs slashed at her thigh. She couldn't move. Both of her arms were pinned to her sides in the suffocating web of tissue.

"Bag!" she gasped. "Can you . . . reach it?"

Josh yanked at her shoulder strap with his left hand, pulling the bag free.

She answered the question in his eyes. "I have . . . another charge. Brought two . . ."

Dizzy with pain, Ventry reached into the sack, closing his grip on the explosive package. "Got it!"

"Red button . . . on the side . . ." Cris struggled to speak. Each word was an effort. "Activates . . . forty seconds."

Josh knew they had no hope of survival now, but at least they could take this hell-thing with them. A better way to die than being ripped apart and devoured.

He pressed the red button.

A loud ticking issued from the device. Incredibly, the train-thing seemed to know its life was in jeopardy. Its shocked mass abruptly drew back, cringing away from the activated explosive charge which dropped to the slimed floor.

Josh and Cris were suddenly released from the jellied tissue.

Dazed, they staggered drunkenly, blood running from a multitude of wounds.

Already ten seconds had ticked away.

Thirty seconds of life remained.

"Out . . ." Josh could barely articulate the words. "Outside . . . *Move!*"

He pushed Cris toward the membrane separating them from the exit.

It had resealed itself.

Josh lowered his head, throwing his body at the rubbery curtain of flesh. He smashed into it, bouncing back.

*Twenty-five seconds.*

"Knife," gasped Cris. "Use the knife."

In his dazed blood fever, Josh had forgotten the hunting knife.

He fumbled at his belt with his right hand. Blood pulsed

steadily from the area of his severed thumb. He couldn't free the knife.

*Twenty seconds.*

Using his left hand, he dragged the weapon lose, turned, driving it into the veined tissue, slashing at the membrane with rapidly diminishing strength.

"Hurry!" Cris urged, agony in her tone.

*Fifteen seconds.*

Now! The curtain parted under his blade—and they plunged through.

Onto the locomotive platform.

The train had now stopped rolling; it was motionless on the rails.

*Ten seconds.*

They dived for the cindered bank, struck ground, rolled.

A searing pain in Ventry's left ankle. Cris reached him. "Twisted it," he said.

"Hurry," Cris told him, dragging him to his feet. "We've only got—"

*Five seconds.*

Ventry struggled forward, but his ankle gave way. He fell, crashing down on his face.

*Too late.*

Cris flung her body across his.

Night became day.

The massive locomotive was lifted from the tracks in a concussion of exploding wood, metal, and flesh.

Gobbets of alien tissue rained down in a hideous shower, covering their lacerated bodies.

# 79

DAY.
Early morning.
Bright sunlight.
A whipping sound above the trees as a helicopter descended.

Sheriff John Longbow stepped from the chopper to survey the devastation around him.

"Christ a'mighty!" he breathed.

And then he saw the two sprawled bodies, moved quickly to them.

Cris Mitchell and Josh Ventry. And they were . . .

. . . *alive!*

Josh opened his eyes and looked up at Longbow. His blood-smeared lips curved into a thin smile.

A smile of triumph.